Love Inspired® SUSPENSE

HIGH
DESERT
HIDEAWAY

JENNA NIGHT

Love Inspired SUSPENSE

Suspenseful romances of danger and faith.

AVAILABLE THIS MONTH

SPECIAL AGENT
Classified K-9 Unit
Valerie Hansen

ROCKY MOUNTAIN SABOTAGE
Jill Elizabeth Nelson

LANCASTER COUNTY RECKONING
Kit Wilkinson

HIDDEN LEGACY
Lynn Huggins Blackburn

HIGH DESERT HIDEAWAY
Jenna Night

DEADLY MEMORIES
Mary Alford

ISBN-13: 978-0-373-45714-4

50599

⬡ EAN

LISATMIFC0617

"Where were you hit?"

Nate quickly unbuckled his seat belt and moved toward her.

Her face was drained of color, her dark brown eyes looking bigger than usual.

When she didn't answer, he started checking her for injuries, carefully brushing aside the bits of safety glass from her side window.

"I'm not hit," she finally said, her voice oddly calm. She had to be in shock. He glanced at the windshield and saw a hole surrounded by a spiderweb of cracks where the bullet had passed through.

Ambush was Nate's first thought. But from where? He twisted in the seat to look in every direction around them, but he couldn't see anybody. "I'm going to unfasten your seat belt."

"Okay." Her voice sounded robotic. He didn't blame her for being scared. He was scared, too. Maybe they were surrounded. Maybe somebody was getting ready to close in on them.

He unbuckled her seat belt and gently tugged down on her arm. "Slide to the floorboard and tuck down as low as you can. Stay out of sight."

Jenna Night comes from a family of Southern-born natural storytellers. Her parents were avid readers and the house was always filled with books. No wonder she grew up wanting to tell her own stories. She's lived on both coasts, but currently resides in the Inland Northwest, where she's astonished by the occasional glimpse of a moose, a herd of elk or a soaring eagle.

Books by Jenna Night

Love Inspired Suspense

Last Stand Ranch
High Desert Hideaway

HIGH DESERT HIDEAWAY

JENNA NIGHT

 HARLEQUIN® LOVE INSPIRED® SUSPENSE

Recycling programs
for this product may
not exist in your area.

LOVE INSPIRED BOOKS

ISBN-13: 978-0-373-45714-4

High Desert Hideaway

www.Harlequin.com

Printed in U.S.A.

Behold, I will do a new thing! Now it shall spring forth;
shall you not know it? I will even make a road
in the wilderness and rivers in the desert.
—Isaiah 43:19

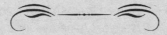

My mom, Esther. My sister, Bonnie. My brother, Roy. My kitty, Miss Loretta. I look forward to seeing you all again. Until then, I'll enjoy the good memories.

Acknowledgments

Thank you to my editor, Elizabeth Mazer, and my agent, Sarah E. Younger, for your generous help and support.

ONE

The cold steel tip of a gun barrel bit into the side of Lily Doyle's neck just below her right ear. The man holding the gun angled it slightly upward, so a single round would have maximum effect.

At least if the worst happened, it would be quick.

Please, Lord, Lily prayed, but she was unable to think of any further words after that. Her knees shook and her breaths came in short, shallow gasps.

"Relax!" the gunman yelled and Lily jumped.

A truck rumbled by on the highway outside the Starlight Mart. "Everybody, just relax!" the gunman yelled again. He'd pulled his dusty gray trucker's hat down low and flipped up the collar of his jean jacket to try and hide his face. Lily didn't know his name, but she did know he'd taken over the convenience store because he wanted to capture her.

The gunman's accomplice, wearing sunglasses and a rust-colored hoodie drawn tight around his face, grabbed an energy drink from a display case. He flung it at the security camera near the cash register where Lily was being held, breaking the camera and sending purplish fizz splattering in every direction. Two wide-eyed store clerks, both looking as if they were barely out of their teens, stood behind the front counter, not far from Lily. They had their hands held up. Hoodie grabbed a second energy drink, threw it and knocked out the camera by the front door.

One of the shoppers screamed.

"Everybody stay where you are," the gunman hollered. "Don't move an inch. Don't touch your phones. Don't try to act smart or you'll find your head exploding like one of them drink cans."

Lily heard a whimpering sound. It came from the trio of high school kids over by the soda cooler.

This wasn't a robbery. Well, not primarily a robbery. Lily had no idea what these two creeps were capable of, but she did know it was her fault the people in this store were in danger. She'd overheard part of a conversation at her new job that she clearly wasn't meant to hear. And the two strangers she'd accidentally heard talking had seen her and come after her.

Now she had to do something. *Nobody's going to ride in on a white horse and save the day, Tiger Lily.* She'd heard her mother say it a thousand times. It had always been true before. It was true now.

Fear squeezed her rib cage, making it hard to breathe. She took the deepest breath she could, forcing her attention away from the crawling sensation of a bead of sweat rolling down the side of her face. She needed to look around. Figure out her options. There *must* be something she could do.

Directly in front of her, a scaled-down baker's rack displayed factory-made muffins, cupcakes and single-serving fruit pies. Through the thick white wires, she could see a wide-eyed woman with her arms wrapped around a boy and girl, maybe five and eight years old, clutching them close to her body.

To the right, midway down the length of cooler doors that covered one wall, stood the trio of teenagers. Slack-jawed and wearing stunned expressions, each one loosely held a neon-colored sports drink as if they'd forgotten they had anything in their hands.

"What are you looking at?" the gunman shouted at Lily as he pulled his arm tighter across the front of her shoulders, forcing her body closer to his. He jammed the tip of his gun harder into her neck, forcing her head to tilt to the side. "You get any smart ideas, you force me to shoot anybody, and their blood will be on your hands." His lips were close to her ear and his hot, damp breath clung sickeningly to the surface of her skin.

Lily's racing heart pounded even harder. The interior of the store started to spin a little and she was afraid she might faint. *Oh, dear Lord. Help!*

She looked through the tall glass windows to the gas pumps outside. Beyond the pumps, a black ribbon of highway wound past the small old store. On the other side of the road, northern Arizona high desert stretched toward jagged mountains. The Starlight Mart sat at a crossroads nearly twenty miles from the nearest town.

A semi rumbled by on the highway but there was no other traffic behind it.

"We're just gonna get everybody together nice and cozy and locked up in some office or storeroom, and then we'll be on our way," the gunman's accomplice called out.

Lily's thoughts turned to news stories of people found murdered in the back rooms of businesses that had been robbed. A chill passed through her body, raising goose bumps on the surface of her skin.

The accomplice pulled a gun out of his hoodie pocket and aimed it at the teenagers, motioning for them to move toward the front of the store. One of the kids tripped over her own feet and fell to her knees, hard. The accomplice laughed.

Lily glanced out the windows again. Her car was pulled up to the front door at a crazy angle, the driver's door still hanging open.

Hoping someone would pull into the parking lot and end this nightmare wasn't much of a plan, but fear and disbelief made it hard to think of anything better.

Lily's entire universe had been upended in less than an hour.

Thirty minutes ago she'd been at work and everything was perfectly normal. Then, twenty-five minutes ago she'd stumbled across a conversation she wasn't meant to hear. Working a little later than usual at her new job as a part-time clerical assistant, she'd walked through an empty office that was adjoined to the break room. Nearly everyone else had already gone home and the building was quiet. She'd heard indistinct voices, but hadn't thought much about it. Then, she was able to make out snippets of conversation and her mind had begun to understand a strange collection of words. *Cops. Cargo. Lay low for a while. Ditch the guns.*

Scared, she'd tried to backtrack through the office, away from the break room and the voices. But she'd bumped into a squeaky rolling office chair, and a man she'd never seen before had yanked open a door and spotted her. He'd demanded to know what she'd heard.

He'd shoved aside the door and started toward her,

cursing while trying to grab her. Startled and scared, she'd run from him. Her phone and purse were still at her desk, but her keys were in her pocket. Afraid there would be no one in the office to help her, she'd raced to her car.

Outside she'd looked around frantically for help as she ran, but she was on her own. She'd flung herself into her car, locked the doors and fired up the engine. Without looking back she'd sped out of the parking lot and shot down the short private road leading to the highway, anxious to get to her home in Copper Mesa.

Shaking and numb with fear, she'd barely caught her breath when she realized her car's low-fuel light was blinking. She'd never make it to Copper Mesa. It was too far. She'd have to head in the opposite direction, toward the crossroads, and hope she had enough fuel to make it to the gas station there.

A couple of minutes later she was pulling off the highway at the Starlight Mart, throwing gravel in a rooster tail behind her. She skidded to a stop right at the front door, jumped out of the car and ran inside, yelling at the startled clerks to call for help. They'd stared at her like her hair was on fire.

She'd forced herself to calm down a little, lower the volume of her voice and try to sound reasonable. But then she'd heard the door behind her being shoved open and the sound of quick footsteps. She'd turned just as the man she'd seen in the office grabbed her hair and yanked her head back. That's when he'd shoved the gun into her neck.

Her brain knew it had only been a few minutes, but it felt as if that gun had been digging into her skin for hours.

Lily looked again at the people in the store, her gaze

settling on the woman with the young children. Their lives were in danger as long as Lily was here.

"I'll go with you," Lily said to the gunman, her voice a shaky whisper. "No trouble." When they got outside, she could break away and run to the highway. Someone driving by might see her and stop. That might be enough to make the gunman and Hoodie let her go while they tried to get away.

The front door of the store opened.

A man walked in. A big guy with shaggy dark blond hair sporting a few sun-bleached streaks. Scruffy beard. Heavy boots. Worn jeans with torn knees, a red T-shirt and a beat-up black leather jacket. He looked like a biker. He wore mirrored sunglasses even though it was now dark outside. He probably wanted to hide his eyes because he was drunk. Or high. After a slight pause, he headed straight for the coolers, toward the section in the back where they kept the soda and beer.

Not the kind of person Lily had had in mind when she'd hoped someone would show up. She turned her head slightly to watch him.

"Don't even think about saying or doing anything." The gunman slid his pistol down so it was hidden, but now it was pointed at the base of Lily's spine. "Make a move and you'll never walk again."

Lily swallowed thickly.

His accomplice moved closer to the teenagers and lowered his gun out of sight.

The biker reached the coolers and peered through the glass as if he was trying to decide what he wanted to buy.

Hurry up! Lily thought. *Get something and get out of here!* He would obviously be more trouble than help.

His sudden appearance had ramped up the tension in the store tenfold. The gunman was now holding Lily's arm in a death grip, his fingers digging deeply into her flesh. His breathing was speeding up, as if he might be getting ready to make a move. The store clerks were getting fidgety, and Lily was worried they might try to do something that would get them killed.

Biker man finally opened a cooler door and grabbed a six-pack of cola-filled cans. Heading toward the cash register, he strode up the aisle toward the man in the hoodie and the group of teenagers. He was tall and broad-shouldered and the cluster of teens moved out of his way.

As he walked past the man in the hoodie, he swung the six-pack and clocked him in the side of the head. In a flash of movement he grabbed the gun from Hoodie's hand just before Hoodie tumbled into a candy rack and knocked it over. Chocolate bars, mints and packs of gum skittered across the floor as the biker reached beneath his jacket. He pulled out his own pistol and pointed it at the gunman who held Lily. "Drop your weapon!"

The gunman loosened his hold on Lily as he raised his gun to fire at the biker.

It was the chance Lily had been hoping for. She jabbed her right elbow straight back, connecting with the gunman's ribs. At the same time she raised her left foot and stomped on his instep. Any second she expected to feel the gun blast into the base of her spine or the back of her head, but the gunman shoved her aside as he fired at the biker.

Two cooler doors exploded and glass fell like jagged rain.

The biker disappeared.

* * *

Deputy Nate Bedford crouched on the floor behind an ice-cream cooler. He peered around the edge of the coffin-shaped container and through some wire display racking, watching the gunman at the counter and the woman he'd held by the arm. The man's unnaturally tight hold on the woman had been the first thing that had caught Nate's attention when he'd walked into the store. Then he'd noticed the odd way everyone was standing still. And the uneasy quiet.

The car parked at the front of the store with the driver's side door hanging open had hinted something might be wrong, too. Or the driver could just be incredibly impatient. Nate had seen it all.

The reflection in the cooler doors as he'd searched for his favorite cola had given him a quick sense of who was where in the store. Who looked terrified, and who looked dangerous and ready to snap. By the time he'd found the drinks he wanted, it was clear he'd have to do something.

Nate was on his way home after spending three months working undercover assisting the Phoenix police department's narcotics unit. The deep undercover assignment had sharpened his observational skills and fine-tuned his ability to read any environment, though the peculiar situation in the Starlight Mart would have been obvious to anybody who was paying attention to their surroundings.

He was exhausted after surviving three months of restless, uneasy sleep every night and his nerves were stretched to their limit thanks to the constant threat of drug-cartel-related violence. He had stopped at the Starlight Mart to pick up a soda to help keep him awake until he got to the Blue Spruce Ranch.

Well, he was awake now.

From his hiding place on the floor, Nate watched the gunman at the counter scanning the store, searching for him. There were large round mirrors in the corners of the ceiling to help detect shoplifters, and reflective glass and steel surfaces everywhere. The gunman was bound to see him any second. Nate shifted his weight and got ready to sprint. Then he heard something. He turned in the direction of the sound.

The teenagers had hit the deck when the gunman started shooting. Now they were getting to their feet. Where did they think they were going?

Nate glanced back toward the front of the store. The woman who was apparently being held hostage by the gunman was also starting to move. Freed from his grasp and shoved to the ground, she'd gotten to her hands and knees and was now crawling toward the front door. Not a good idea. Not yet. The guy in the hoodie Nate had whacked still lay on the floor, moaning. The gunman was obviously spooked and itching to shoot again. Nate had experience with edgy, violent people. This was a textbook definition of an explosive situation.

The woman was still crawling. Her dark hair was tied back, but a few strands had worked loose and fallen around her face. She wore black-framed glasses and looked smart, like a librarian. She looked familiar, too, but Nate couldn't place her. It could be his mind playing tricks on him. Undercover work always left him edgy and suspicious. It took a little time to transition back into his normal self. Staying up at the Blue Spruce Ranch for a few days would help with that. It always did.

The woman was gutsy, Nate had to give her that. Maybe too gutsy. Any second now she would get too far. The gunman would be afraid she'd escape. He'd panic and shoot her. Nate had to do something to draw the gunman's fire away from her.

He took a deep breath to steady his nerves and slowly rose up.

The sound of rapid footsteps jerked away his attention. Something screamed, like the sound of a train squealing to a stop, and a whoosh of cooler air swirled through the small store. The clerks were running out the back door, the teenagers right behind them. Someone had pushed open the emergency exit and activated the alarm.

Nate looked over his shoulder. The guy in the hoodie he'd knocked out earlier was no longer on the floor. Nate couldn't see him anywhere.

At the front of the store the gunman grabbed the woman and yanked her to her feet. Then he looked around, wild-eyed, and fired a couple of random shots into the store, hitting a pyramid of salsa jars and a light fixture that sent sparks spraying to the floor. While Nate took cover, the gunman started toward the front door, pulling the woman with him.

Nate couldn't return fire. The woman was in the way. "Throw down your gun," Nate yelled, figuring the gunman probably couldn't hear him over the screaming drone of the alarm.

The gunman fired a shot in Nate's direction. Then he backed toward the door, looking over his shoulder several times, dragging the woman with him. Finally, he reached the threshold. He hesitated, then shoved the woman into the store while he turned and ran outside.

Nate sprang up and ran after him.

The sky had gone from dark blue to pitch-black while Nate was inside. Buzzing white security lights shone over the gas pumps, but the fleeing gunman was nowhere in sight. He must have taken off into the wildland.

Nate jogged across the crumbling asphalt, continuing around the back of the store, just in case the bad guys had gone that way. He came across the high school kids and clerks who'd escaped out the back door. They were clustered in small groups. Some were crying, some were hugging each other. Nearly all were on their cell phones.

Nate tucked his gun back under his jacket. "Did anybody see where either of those two guys went?"

The kids glanced at each other and shook their heads.

"I called 911," one of the clerks offered. Nate could already hear sirens. A couple of cars rolled by on the highway, red taillights glowing in the night, but there was no way to tell if either car held the escaping thugs.

Nate went back inside the store with one of the clerks and they disarmed the shrieking alarm. Blue and red flashing lights spilled through the front window as the patrol cars pulled into the parking lot.

Nate walked all through the store, checking the restrooms, office and storage areas to make sure the man in the hoodie wasn't hiding anywhere. There was no sign of him. He must have slipped out the back door when everybody else ran.

Deputies cautiously entered the store. They recognized Nate and he waved them in. "Two guys held everybody in the store hostage and then got away," Nate told the senior deputy. "I guess it was a robbery. I'm not sure. I got here in the middle of it." He gave their descriptions. "Wish I could tell you if they're on foot or driving, but I don't know."

"We'll get everybody out looking." The senior deputy, David Cooper, keyed his collar mic to speak to Dispatch. Meanwhile the other deputies fanned out to do their own search of the premises and get started collecting witness information.

"The gunman at the front counter was hanging on to that lady over there pretty tightly," Nate said to Cooper after he'd finished talking to Dispatch. He gestured toward the dark-haired woman in the glasses who stood by the main entrance, her arms wrapped across her stomach as she stared at the ground. "I couldn't tell if they were after her in particular for some reason, but I'd like to find out."

Nate strode over to her. "Are you all right?"

Her head jerked up. She looked at him, wide-eyed, and tried to take a step back. But she was already pressed against the glass at the front of the store and there was nowhere for her to go.

"The bad guys are gone," Nate quickly added. "I just wanted to make sure you weren't hurt. The medics are outside. Maybe you should get checked out."

"I'm okay," she finally answered in a low voice. She blew out a shaky breath. "I thought they were going to kill me."

"You're safe now." Nate had been through some terrifying situations in his life. Dwelling on all the horrific things that could have happened never did him any good. Focusing on what went right, and thanking God, did.

"How did all this get started?" Nate asked. "Do you know those guys?"

"I've seen them before but I don't know them." She reached up to tuck a few stray tendrils of hair behind her ears and recrossed her arms. "I was in the wrong place at the wrong time. They must have thought I was going to turn them in to the police or something."

"I've got this." Cooper walked up and gave Nate a look that clearly said "go away."

It was standard operating procedure to separate witnesses when gathering statements after an incident like this. Nate knew that, but he wasn't used to being only a witness. He was used to being a cop and taking control.

"Go find Gibson and give him your statement," Cooper added. "And Sheriff Wolfsinger is on his way. He's going to want to talk to you."

"Right." Nate glanced back at the dark-haired woman, bugged by the thought that he knew her from somewhere. He should have asked her name. He'd find out eventually.

TWO

Lily sat down in the driver's seat of her car, stretched across the passenger seat and stuck her hand down between the seat and the door, digging around for loose change so she could buy some gasoline and get home.

Deputy Cooper had taken her statement. She'd told him everything, from overhearing bits and pieces of a conversation between strangers to being chased here to the Starlight Mart and held at gunpoint. She'd explained to him that she hadn't even heard enough to understand what the men were talking about, and she'd given him the name and location of her new employer, though she didn't have her phone with her and couldn't remember the phone number. Finally, the deputy handed her his card and told her he'd follow up with her tomorrow morning.

Now she had her car pulled up to the gas pumps outside the Starlight Mart. She worked three part-time jobs and typically got her lunch at a fast-food drive-thru window. Sometimes she dropped her change on the floor or tossed it onto the passenger seat when she was in a hurry. Maybe there was enough to buy the gasoline she needed to get her home. If not, she'd have to walk back into the Starlight Mart and try to borrow the money from somebody.

Home. That's all she wanted to think about right now. The comfortable old house she'd grown up in. The dogs. And most of all, her mom. Mom would help her hold herself together.

She didn't want to think about what had just happened to her in the Starlight Mart, or what might have happened if that biker hadn't shown up. She absolutely didn't want to dwell on the terrifying possibility that the gunman and his accomplice might track her down tomorrow or the next day. The second time they found her they'd probably drag her out into an isolated expanse of scrub brush and finish the job without witnesses or anyone getting in their way.

She would let herself process what had happened to her after she got home. Right now she would swallow her fear because that's what you did with fear. Lily had learned that at a young age. When trouble comes—and it always does—you choke back your fear and you take care of the job at hand. You do your crying later.

That's what Lily's mom, Kate, did all those years ago when Lily's father died. She'd pulled herself together. And she kept doing that in the years that followed because money was tight and trouble was never very far away.

Lily only found a couple of dimes in the space beside the seat, so she sat up and opened the glove box. She shoved aside her car registration, a few aged ketchup packets and a collection of plastic forks from fast-food restaurants, and finally found a few more coins. Altogether they totaled less than three dollars. Not nearly enough to get her where she wanted to go.

One of the terrified sobs Lily had choked back while that gun bit into her skin rose up in her throat and escaped as a cross between a hiccup and a gasp. Tears burned her eyes. Her body began to tremble.

No, she commanded herself. *You will not do this. Not now.*

"Where do you think you're going?"

The sound of the biker's voice startled her and she dropped her coins. They rolled under the seat. Fear turned into fury in an instant. She'd been terrorized and pushed around more than enough today.

She got out of her car and slammed the door shut, then turned and glared up at the biker. He was definitely big. He'd taken off his dark glasses and she could see his eyes. Cold, unemotional steel-gray. Why was he even talking to her? She didn't want to know him. And he certainly wasn't going to keep her from going home. Not after all she'd been through tonight. It didn't matter how big he was.

She held his gaze for several seconds and then felt her anger drain away just a little. The man had saved her life, after all. She should probably thank him for what he'd done. Unfortunately for him, she wasn't in a particularly generous mood at the moment. "What do you want?" she snapped, just barely managing to sound civil.

He crossed his arms over his chest and tilted his head slightly. "You look like you're trying to leave. Sheriff Wolfsinger arrived a few minutes ago. You need to stay and talk to him."

"I already gave my statement."

"If you talk to him maybe you'll remember some new details."

Lily scoffed. "What are you, a cop?"

"As a matter of fact, I am."

He couldn't be serious.

Apparently he was.

He took out an ID from his back pocket, complete with an Oso County sheriff's department badge, and showed it to her.

"'Nathan Bedford,'" she read aloud from his ID. "That name sounds familiar." She turned back to him. His eyes narrowed, as if he didn't believe her. She didn't care if he did or not. But his cynical expression goaded her. And then she remembered how she knew him. "Cottonwood High School. You hung out with Joseph Suh."

His hardened expression gave way just a little. "I was friends with him for a long time," he said. "You look familiar. What's your name?"

"Lily Doyle. And I wasn't exactly friends with him. I tutored him in English composition." She'd hung around with a totally different crowd than Nate and Joseph when they were all in high school. And every day after school, she'd had a job stocking shelves in a grocery store. If she wasn't in class or at work, she was either studying or sleeping. She hadn't had much time for friends.

"Pip-squeak," he said after a few seconds.

"I beg your pardon?"

"That's the nickname Joseph gave you. Because you were a couple of years younger than us and kind of small."

"Oh." Had Joseph really called her Pip-squeak behind her back? She'd had fond memories of working with Joseph. He'd told her she needed to lighten up and he was always trying to make her laugh. He came from a nice family. His mom made sure Lily had a snack whenever she came to their house to tutor him.

"Joseph said you did a good job," Nate added. "His mom made him sign up for peer tutoring and he was mad at first, but if it wasn't for your help, he might not have graduated."

Lily felt a lump in her throat. For some reason, now that Nate was speaking to her a little more kindly, it was harder to keep her emotions in check.

"I haven't seen Joseph in a long time," Lily finally said. "I know he enlisted in the army. I hope he's doing okay."

"Deployed to the Middle East three times," Nate said evenly. "Made it through two of them."

"Oh."

The barrier Lily had built around her emotions dissolved in an instant. Tears collected in her eyes and then ran down her cheeks. Her shoulders started to shake and her nose started to run. She wiped at her face with the back of her hand.

Nate grabbed a paper towel from the dispenser attached to a pole between the gas pumps and handed it to her. The thick brown paper was meant for cleaning windshields and it was rough on her nose. She used it anyway.

Leaning against her car, she let the tears fall because this time she knew she couldn't stop them. Part of her choking emotion was simply the terror of the day catching up with her. But sharp sadness over the death of Joseph pushed her over the top. What a horrible reminder that terrible things happened to people all the time.

Finally she calmed down a little, took a breath and

sighed. She wadded up the paper towel and tossed it into a trash can. Nate quickly got her another one. She didn't really need it, but just throwing it away seemed spiteful so she put it into her pocket.

Trying not to be obvious, she stole another glance at him. Nate Bedford had always been easy on the eyes. But she didn't ever remember him looking this scruffy. And now he was a deputy sheriff? She would have been less surprised to learn he was an inmate somewhere.

"Thank you," she finally said. "Thank you for saving my life in there."

Nate nodded. "You're welcome."

He looked past her shoulder into the darkness surrounding the Starlight Mart.

A chill wind kicked up and Lily rubbed her arms.

"It's cold out here." Nate flipped up the collar on his leather jacket and turned to her. "Are you ready to go back inside the store to talk to the sheriff?"

"Yes." Since he was asking instead of telling her, Lily figured she could work with him.

"Good. Try to remember every single detail you possibly can. You never know what might help. I'll see if I can join in the hunt to track down those two idiots and make them pay for what they did."

Inside the Starlight Mart, Oso County Sheriff Ben Wolfsinger had taken up his usual role as the calm center in the midst of the storm. A slender, bronze-skinned man with gray shot through the black hair at his temples, Wolfsinger wasn't a physically imposing man. But his confident demeanor and calm voice lent him a presence that drew people's attention.

Wolfsinger saw Nate and quirked an eyebrow. "Bedford. I heard you were here. Why aren't you at home in Painted Rock getting some rest?"

"I decided to go to the ranch instead. I stopped here to get something to drink on the way." He introduced Lily to the sheriff.

"You're the lady we've been hearing about from our eyewitnesses." Wolfsinger reached out a hand and rested it on her shoulder. "I'm so sorry about what happened to you."

Nate watched Lily look into Wolfsinger's eyes, take a deep breath, exhale and relax her shoulders a little. She had scratches on her neck and a bruise darkening the top of her right cheek. Thin red lines across her forehead and chin marked spots where something sharp, perhaps shattered glass from the cooler, or pieces of broken lightbulb, had sliced across the surface of her skin.

Thinking about the creeps who had hurt her made Nate's stomach tighten.

As an elected official, Sheriff Wolfsinger could pull out some impressive political skills when necessary, but he was also a decent and compassionate human being. Which was probably why he kept getting reelected without doing any actual campaigning.

A few minutes later they were sitting in the store's office. Nate and Wolfsinger listened to Lily finish telling her story of what had happened. Nate was intrigued.

Lily worked at a trucking company—Torrent Trucking.

A sophisticated theft ring had been stealing cargo trailers along the highways crisscrossing Oso County for quite a while. It was a multistate problem and an interagency task force had been formed while Nate was away. Nate already knew he would be attached to the task force when he returned to duty, thanks to the specialized training he'd received as a military policeman investigating large-scale theft of military property. He was itching to get started.

"We need to talk to Bryan Torrent," Nate said to the sheriff. The owner of Torrent Trucking was well known in Copper Mesa. His parents had started several enterprises that Bryan inherited. Torrent Trucking was the only one still in business.

"*I* will talk to Bryan Torrent," Wolfsinger said, turning to Nate. "*You* go on to the ranch. Tell Bud and Ellen I said hello. Take your week off. Get some rest. There'll be plenty for you to do when you report back to work."

"Yes, sir." Nate stood. "Are you going to talk to Bryan Torrent tonight? He must know the two guys we're looking for."

"Maybe not," Lily said slowly.

Nate turned to her, a quicksilver flash of suspicion squirming in his gut. "Why do you say that?" What did she know and what was she hiding?

"I've only been working there a few weeks. Part-time. But I've never seen Mr. Torrent in the office. He doesn't come around much." She crossed her arms and let out a small, deflated laugh. "I thought working there would be a great opportunity."

She glanced down for a minute, then looked directly into Nate's eyes. "Torrent Trucking doesn't just dispatch trucks and drivers. There are warehouses on the property. Sometimes truckload deliveries are brought in, the pallets are broken down and the items are delivered locally. Sometimes semis bring in an entire trailer full of freight that's kept in storage until it's picked up by another driver, who will complete the delivery.

"There are all kinds of drivers in and out of there. Most of them aren't Torrent Trucking employees. Drivers are welcome to take a break in the break room, where there's hot coffee and some vending machines. The men I overheard talking, the ones who chased me here to the Starlight Mart, were in that break room." She pressed her lips together and shook her head. "If they actually worked for Torrent Trucking, I would have seen them before."

"I'll call Mr. Torrent in a few minutes and find out what he knows," Wolfsinger said. "We'll go to his business and talk to as many people as we can." He got to his feet and turned to Nate. "If the men we're looking for are not employees, then we'll get a list of all the drivers who've been in and out of there in the last month."

Someone knocked on the office door and called out to the sheriff.

"I need to get back out there." Wolfsinger turned to Lily. "I'll have a deputy drive you home."

"I can drive you home," Nate said to Lily a couple of minutes later as they walked out of the store and into the parking lot.

"No thanks, I can drive myself."

"I can bring you back tomorrow to get your car." Despite her brave front, her nerves had to be shattered after what she'd just been through. This wasn't a good time for her to be driving. And maybe Nate felt a little bit of a personal connection to her now because she had known Joseph.

Growing up, Joseph was the only friend Nate had who didn't make jokes about how drunk Nate's mom got or how crazy she acted. Joseph and his family were always warm and welcoming. Maybe it was a stretch, but it felt as if seeing Lily safely home would be a way of doing something for him.

Nate was heading toward Copper Mesa to get to the ranch, anyway. He was also looking forward to sleeping late for the first time in weeks, but he would get up early in the morning and drive into Copper Mesa to get Lily and take her back to the Starlight Mart to fetch her car if that's what she wanted. And that would be the end of it. No further personal involvement or obligation.

"You've been through a lot," Nate said. "I think it would be wise for you to let me take you home. I'm heading in that direction anyway."

She looked as if she was going to argue, but then blew out a breath. "Maybe you're right. Let me go move my car so it's out of the way."

Nate held out his hand. "Give me your keys. I'll move it for you."

Inside Nate's truck, Lily sat pressed so close to the passenger-side door that he was afraid she might try to jump out. The apparent shock that had helped her keep herself composed after that one brief crying jag earlier was starting to wear off. He could tell by her slumped shoulders and the pinched expression on her face.

Thank You, Lord, for getting us through this. Nate couldn't always pray in the midst of trouble, but he always prayed eventually. For help. For healing. For guidance or to give thanks. He couldn't do his job without it.

Before turning left out of the parking lot and heading toward Copper Mesa, Nate glanced right toward the intersecting highway that led to Painted Rock. His apartment was in Painted Rock. He'd been exiled to the substation up there several months ago. By the time he left for his assignment in Phoenix, he'd managed to make a few friends and develop a fondness for the little town. But he still wasn't anxious to return to his empty apartment there.

"So, you're a cop now," Lily said after they'd pulled out onto the highway and driven a few miles in silence. "From what I remember in high school, I would have expected you to end up on the other side of the law."

"Yeah, there was a time when I would have expected that, too."

The highway they followed passed through a stretch of scrubby flatland. In the wash of headlights, it looked like the bottom of an empty sea.

Nate's life had felt empty from the time he was a kid. He'd had one picture of his dad, a United States marine who was killed protecting an embassy in South America. Nate's mother, Brenda, had turned to alcohol to deal with her grief. Oftentimes she went on benders and Nate wouldn't see her for days at a time.

In his midteens he finally moved in with his Uncle Bud and Aunt Ellen at their ranch, the Blue Spruce. Bud and Nate's mom were brother and sister. Bud offered multiple times to help Brenda sober up and get her life together, but she wasn't interested. She didn't want him involved in her son's life, either. Eventually, against Brenda's will but with the insistence of the state of Arizona, Bud got custody of his nephew.

At first it was hard living by Bud and Ellen's rules. Nate was a kid back then, and nearly everybody acts like a jerk when they're a teenager, but it was still embarrassing to think about how he'd behaved.

Nate cleared his throat. "It took a while, but I finally got my head on straight. I enlisted in the army and served as a military policeman. When my enlistment ended, I knew I wanted to come home and work as a cop." It was the only way he knew to pay back the people who'd helped him over the years.

The highway rose in elevation and pine trees began to appear on the sides of the road. They rounded a bend and the town of Copper Mesa came into view. Streetlights gave it the appearance of a blazing crown in the darkness.

"All right, which way?" Nate asked as they got closer to town. He glanced in his mirrors. There'd been a couple of vehicles behind them for a while. Not much he could do but keep an eye on them. It could be nothing. If they followed his turns once he got into town, he'd know they meant trouble.

"Head toward Cottonwood High," Lily said. "I'm living in the old neighborhood. I had to move back into my mom's house."

"Do you want to borrow my phone and call her?" Nate asked. He'd offered her the use of his phone earlier, but she'd turned him down.

"I don't want to wake her up if she's asleep," Lily said. "She's been battling bronchitis for a few days. She has asthma, so it's kind of a big deal."

Nate kept his eyes on the road, but he picked up his phone from where it was sitting on the bench seat and held it out to her. If the bad guys really were connected to the place where she worked, they might have access to her home address. He didn't want to mention that possibility because he didn't want to send her into a panic without reason. "I think you should call your mom."

She hesitated, then took the phone and punched in a few digits. Soon she was talking to her mom and giving Nate hand gestures showing him where to turn.

Hearing her mom's voice seemed to relax her a little. It sounded as if everything was okay. She didn't mention what had happened at the Starlight Mart, but he didn't blame her. Some things were better shared in person.

Nate kept checking his mirrors. One car stayed on his tail, which worried him. But then Lily directed him to make a turn and the car behind them kept going straight.

"We're almost home," Lily said into the phone while pointing Nate toward a house at the end of the road. "I mean *I'm* almost home," she quickly said into the phone. "I'll be there in a couple of minutes." She disconnected.

Nate pulled into the driveway of the house. The porch light was on and a couple of lights burned upstairs. It was in the older part of Copper Mesa, a little run-down-looking, and it backed up to the ravine that meandered through town.

Nate cut the engine and opened his door.

"What are you doing?" Lily asked, getting out.

"I'm walking you to your door." He got out and came around to meet her.

"Thank you, but I'd rather you didn't." She bit her bottom lip for a few seconds. "It's just that I've already put my mom through a lot lately. Seeing you might make her heart stop. Not in a good way," she added with a slight smile.

Nate looked down at his leather jacket and torn jeans. He ran his hand over his beard. When he'd gotten the green light to leave Phoenix and go home, he'd just jammed. No cleaning up his appearance first, no haircut or shave. "I'll tell her I'm a deputy sheriff," he said. "Show her my ID."

"I realize you think that would be comforting, but it

won't make her feel better. She'll realize something bad happened if I need a cop to drive me home."

"Okay." Nate glanced up and down the street. "Sheriff Wolfsinger will have deputies driving by throughout the night while they're on patrol. I'll hang out here until the first one shows up so I can fill him or her in on the details. Let them know one of the guys they're looking for should have soda can–sized bruises on the side of his face."

Lily managed a small laugh despite her apparent exhaustion. "Thanks."

"You're welcome. Good night." He watched her turn, walk up the garden path to the front door and step inside the house.

He got back into his truck, pulled out of the driveway, drove around the block and then parked midway down the street, where he had a good view of the house. The chilly, late-autumn wind started to pick up again, shaking leaves and branches around her house near the windows and the front door.

Something caught his eye. Movement by a corner window. He stared at it, trying to determine if it was something to be concerned about, or if it was just a shifting shadow.

THREE

Lily's muscles felt stiff and sore as she walked through the front door of her mom's house. She'd experienced nearly every emotion possible over the last few hours, as well as the physical reactions that went with each one. No wonder she felt like she'd just gone a couple of rounds with a three-hundred-pound prizefighter.

The chilly fall wind loosened wisps of hair from her ponytail, and brushed the skin around her face like itchy, impatient fingers. She smoothed her disheveled hair as she walked through the small entryway in the house. The kitchen, which was to the left, had a dining area with room for a small round table, two chairs and not much else. The living room was to the right, with its comfy, well-worn and unmatched furniture.

The curtains in the window on the far side of the living room twitched.

A furry snout pushed through the spot where the two pieces of fabric met. Another snout poked through beside it and then wagging tails batted the fabric back and forth. Two miniature dachshunds jumped down from the windowsill. Abby and Beatrice. Their dark eyes shone with light that spilled into the living room from the kitchen.

"Hi, girls!" Lily kneeled to let the little pooches kiss her.

She was finally home. And *Deputy* Nate Bedford had helped her get here. That was still hard to believe. Her entire experience tonight was hard to believe.

Abby and Beatrice whined joyfully. "I'm happy to see you, too." Lily picked them up for a squeeze and gave them each a kiss on the head before setting them back down.

Once the dogs were settled, Lily took a minute to take a breath and compose herself before going upstairs to tell her mom what had happened at the Starlight Mart.

Kate Doyle had worked very hard at multiple jobs over the years while Lily was growing up, providing for the two of them and keeping a roof over their heads. The memory had made Lily's failure and subsequent return home from college all the more bitter.

She was supposed to have made something of herself by finally earning her degree after numerous delays. The plan had been to get a well-paying job and pay her mom back for all her sacrifices over the years. Kick a little extra money her mom's way so she could take a break and put her feet up now and then. Not that her mom had ever asked for such a thing.

It was Lily's goal to make her mom's life easier and she had failed. By moving back home, she'd added to her mom's burdens. She'd been forced to leave college just a couple of months ago, and now she had to tell her mom she'd been held hostage and nearly killed.

She was tempted not to tell her mom about what had happened to keep her from worrying. But Kate was a social butterfly—definitely not an attribute Lily had inherited—and somehow she would find out. Might as well get it over with.

Lily walked through the shadowy living room and up the narrow stairs. "Come on, girls!"

Abby and Beatrice bolted past her, their ears flapping like proud wiener-dog flags as they led the way.

Her mom had a sitting room next to her bedroom. It was really just a small bedroom, but she'd put in a sofa, a comfy chair and a TV.

Lily hesitated when she reached the top of the stairs, trying to decide if she should ease into the details of what had happened or just blurt it out.

The dogs ran ahead of her down the hall and into the sitting room. Over the sound of the TV, Lily heard her mom say, "What have you two girls been up to?"

"I'm home," Lily called out, trying to sound upbeat as she walked down the hall.

Her mom was stretched out on the sofa, a hand-crocheted multicolored afghan pulled up to her chin. She had to feel terrible. It took a lot to keep Kate Doyle down. A tissue box sat within reach on an end table. A few foil-wrapped chocolates trailed along the arm of the couch.

"Hi, honey, you're home late." Her mom sat up. She started to brush her hair away from her face and then suddenly froze. "What happened?"

Lily caught her reflection in a wall mirror. Tear-smeared mascara had left dark circles around her eyes. Her blouse was rumpled and dirt covered the bottom of her slacks where she'd crawled across the floor. She had a bruise and some small cuts on her face.

How could she not have noticed that earlier?

She walked to a chair and sat down, smoothing her hair and straightening her blouse. In this warm, safe, cozy room where Lily could finally let her guard down, the icy terror that came from having a gun shoved into her neck wormed its way back into her consciousness. Her hands started to tremble.

"The good news is I'm okay," Lily said, her voice a little shaky.

Kate turned off the TV, swung her legs around so her feet were on the floor and dropped the remote onto the couch cushion beside her. "Why wouldn't you be okay?"

In a wavering voice Lily told her mom what had happened, everything from overhearing the conversation at work to Nate Bedford seeing her home.

"Well, you're not going back to work at that trucking company." Her mom crossed her arms over her chest.

Not exactly the comforting response Lily had hoped for, but Kate typically turned practical when she was upset. Lily stood up, walked over and sat next to her mom on the sofa. Kate put an arm around her and pulled her close.

"So, Nate Bedford, huh?" her mom said after they'd sat together in silence for a couple of minutes. Kate didn't know Nate personally, but his mother's drunken antics were well-known throughout town. In the quiet, Lily could hear the wind outside rattle tree branches against the side of the house. "Nate's really a sheriff's deputy now?" her mom added. "Good for him."

"Yeah, I didn't recognize him at first." And if he hadn't shown up when he did, there was no telling what might have happened.

"His poor mom was one tortured soul. And it seemed as if she was determined to drag Nate down with her." Kate shook her head. "It's amazing to see what God can turn to good. I'm going to track that boy down and thank him for helping you."

He might still have been outside watching the house, but more likely he'd headed up to his aunt and uncle's place, the well-known Blue Spruce Ranch. Bud and Ellen Wells had done a lot of good work in the community over the years, much of it with troubled teens. Nate was eventually one of the teens they helped.

"You might get a chance to see Nate in the morning," Lily said. "I left my car at the Starlight Mart and my purse and phone are at work. He's going to take me to get them."

Kate turned to her daughter with a slight smile.

"What?" Lily shook her head, feeling her cheeks warm. "It's not like that, Mom. It's his job to help people. That's all it is."

And that was all it was ever going to be.

Nate had been completely professional. He had no personal interest in her other than as the mutual acquaintance of a beloved old friend. And Lily had a life to rebuild after her engagement had come to an abrupt end and her carefully crafted plans crumbled like an imploded high-rise building. She worked lots of hours with no time for a personal life these days and that's exactly how she wanted it.

After the pain and humiliation she'd been through, mind-numbing work was exactly what she needed.

Her mom hadn't eaten dinner yet and Lily was hungry, too. "I'm going to heat up some soup." Lily had made a pot of chicken noodle soup from scratch the night before. "Do you want me to bring you a bowl?"

"After what you've been through, I should get it," her mom said, her breath sounding wheezy.

"I can get it."

"Thanks, honey." Kate patted the cushion beside her

on the couch. Abby and Beatrice jumped up to cuddle with her. She picked up the remote and turned on the TV.

Downstairs, Lily got the pot of homemade soup out of the fridge and ladled some into a couple of bowls. A mental image of the men at the Starlight Mart, determined to grab her and most likely kill her, flashed through her mind. Her hands started to shake and she spilled some soup. *Everything is okay. It's over. I'm fine.* She took a steadying breath.

Doors and windows. Were they all locked? Probably not.

She put a bowl in the microwave, set it to heat for three minutes and hit the start button. Then she went to check the front door. Yep, it was locked. She turned to face the living room. Through a thin curtain, she saw shadowy black branches wave outside the windows.

Except for one branch that remained still. Something about it didn't look right.

Lily stared into the darkness for a moment. Slowly she realized she was looking at the outline of a man. Her breath caught in her throat. The man wasn't outside the window. He was in the house. In the living room. Standing right there in the corner.

Her first attempt to scream came out as a ragged exhalation. Terrified, she felt as if she was caught in a nightmare, unable to make a sound. The man took a step out of the shadows, toward her, and she could see he was one of the men from the Starlight Mart. The one in the hoodie.

He was pointing a pistol at her. He glanced upstairs toward the blare of the TV, then turned back to her. "Don't make a sound."

"What do you want?" she asked, finally finding her voice.

"Let's go."

"Where?"

He motioned with his gun toward the back of the house, where the door in the utility room led outside. That was probably how he got in. Lily and her mom often left a window open in that room when they ran the dryer. And they were both bad about remembering to close it.

"Move!" Hoodie shoved her.

"I didn't hear anything that could get you in trouble," Lily said, taking a couple of stumbling steps while her heart hammered in her chest. "I just heard voices. Nothing specific."

"Get moving or we'll take your mother along, too."

He wanted to get her outside and into a car. Lily couldn't let that happen. It would be the end of everything.

He shoved her again. Edging toward panic, she reached for a potted plant on a shelf. If she flung something heavy against the wall and made a loud noise, maybe the dogs would hear it and start barking. Her mom would hear the racket and call the police.

Hoodie twisted her arm, hard, and she dropped the potted plant with a dull thud. So much for that plan.

They reached the utility room and she saw the open window. She also saw a mop propped against the wall. Hoodie loosened his grip slightly as he reached for the handle on the door leading outside. Lily took her chance. She kicked his knee. While he was off balance she grabbed the mop, whirled around and smacked him on the side of the head with it.

He dropped his gun. It clattered to the floor and they both reached for it. He jabbed an elbow toward her face, clipping her cheek, and she was knocked back. She dropped the mop. Then he got the gun.

Lily quickly crawled to a bucket of dry laundry detergent and grabbed a handful. Hoodie turned to her and she flung it into his face.

Cursing, he clawed at his eyes with one hand.

Afraid he might squeeze the trigger if she tried to grab his gun, Lily reached for the mop and struck him again. This time Hoodie slumped to the ground. He was out cold.

Footsteps pounded up the back porch steps. Nate must have been watching the house. Relief washing over her, Lily got to her feet and yanked open the door.

It wasn't Nate standing there. It was the man who'd held a gun on her at the Starlight Mart. Lily's heart sank. He had her again.

Nate crouched down low and crept alongside the house.

Lily's mom had called 911. She'd reported strange noises in her house and that her dogs were growling. She was afraid someone had come after her daughter.

Nate was afraid of that, too. Dispatch had let him know what was happening and that the responding deputies were a couple minutes out. Nate knew better than to rush in, but he couldn't just wait in his truck.

Peering around the corner of the house, he saw the gunman from the gas station on the back steps. He was holding Lily by the upper arm and dragging her out of the house. The terrified expression on her face struck Nate like a punch to his chest. *Enough*. Lily Doyle had been through enough. And that idiot holding her was not going to get away with what he'd done.

Nate had the advantage and he intended to make the most of it. The gunman wasn't looking around. He probably thought he was home free. He did, however, have that gun. Trying to take a shot at him was too risky. Nate could miss and hit Lily. Or the gunman could shoot her.

Calm, cool, steady. That's how Nate had to handle this.

At ease working in the shadows, he pressed into the side of the house and took one quiet step and then another. He covered the final short distance in a burst of speed. The gunman turned in surprise just as Nate grabbed his gun hand and landed a cross punch to the side of his head. The gunman dropped like a sack of wet sand.

Eyes wide and filled with fear, Lily swung her fists wildly. Nate had to duck a couple of times before she realized he wasn't another attacker.

"Are you all right?" Nate asked when she finally stopped swinging. He put his hands on her shoulders, holding her at arm's length while scanning her body for injuries.

"Someone's in the house," she said, trying to catch her breath. "Utility room."

Nate hesitated, reluctant to turn his back on the man he'd just knocked unconscious.

"My mom's in the house, too," Lily said, sounding panicky and tugging on his arm. "Hurry!"

Inside the house he found the man in the hoodie lying unconscious on the utility room floor.

"I hit him with the mop," Lily said.

Nate felt the corners of his lips tug upward in an admiring grin. "Good work." He picked up the man's gun and tucked it into his back pocket. Lily got some twine out of a storage cabinet and Nate tied the man's hands behind his back.

Two little dogs not much bigger than mosquitoes ran into the utility room from the living room. A uniformed deputy followed them. A woman wrapped in an afghan walked in behind the deputy.

"Honey, are you okay?" the woman asked Lily after a racking coughing fit.

"I'm okay, Mom." Lily hugged her mom and then introduced her to Nate.

"Thank you for saving my daughter's life," Kate Doyle said. "I'd offer to shake your hand, but I'm fighting bronchitis."

"I think your daughter saved her own life." He turned to the deputy. "There's another bad guy out back."

"No, there isn't." A second deputy walked into the utility room through the back door. "Sorry, Nate. If you had somebody out there, he's long gone. Probably jumped into the ravine and took off. We'll start looking for him." He walked off, speaking into his collar mic.

The man who'd held the gun on her at the store had gotten away. *Again.* Disgusted with himself, Nate shook his head.

One of the little mosquito dogs, the one with a tiny white blaze in the center of her chest, stepped up to sniff the hem of Nate's jeans. Her bone-shaped metallic tag said her name was Abby. Nate reached down to give her a scratch on the head. When she rolled up her eyes to look at him, he was pretty sure she was disappointed in what she saw. Nate didn't blame her.

The man in the hoodie started to stir. The uniformed deputy took off the twine and cuffed him, then patted him down. He found a folded switchblade in his back pocket and a keychain in the front pocket. That was it. No wallet. No ID. Not even a phone. He started to regain consciousness. Nate and the deputy pulled him to a sitting position.

"What's your name?" Nate asked.

The deputy had already tugged back the man's hood, revealing short curly brown hair, thick eyebrows and a soda can–sized bruise across the side of his face. He was maybe in his early thirties. Powdery white laundry detergent streaked his face and the front of his shirt. He squinted his red, watery eyes and frowned at Nate. "Who are you?" His gaze shifted nervously back and forth between Nate and the deputy. "You're that guy who hit me with soda cans in the store."

"Do you recognize this guy from anywhere?" Nate asked Lily. "Maybe you've seen him someplace other than work?" He turned to her and she shook her head. When he turned back to the thug, he saw him staring at Lily. The man's confused scowl had morphed into a bold, predatory stare.

Lily visibly blanched and her eyes grew wide with fear.

"Hey!" Nate snapped at the thug, drawing the man's attention back to himself. "Who are you? Who are you working for?"

The man cursed at him and then looked away, making it clear he wouldn't answer any further questions.

The deputy placed him under arrest and read him his rights, then left with plans to take him to the hospital to get checked out before hauling him to the county jail.

Lily sat down in the living room with the second deputy, who'd returned to the house and was ready to take down her statement. Meanwhile Lily's mom made a call and a few minutes later Kate's cousin, Penny, showed up to offer the women comfort and support.

While his fellow deputy was wrapping things up, Nate mentally rehashed everything that had happened this evening. If those two thugs could find out where Lily lived that quickly *and* they were desperate enough to try to grab her at home, she was in even greater danger than he'd thought. She was going to need something more substantial than the hand-holding her mother and cousin could provide.

Lily's mom had brought out a container of homemade cookies and brewed some coffee. By the time the remaining deputy had taken care of business and gone on his way, there was nothing left but coffee mugs stacked in the kitchen sink and a few butter-pecan cookie crumbs on the kitchen counter.

"Why don't you two pack some clothes and spend the night at my place?" Penny asked Lily and Kate.

"You should go with your cousin," Nate said to Lily's mom. He turned to Lily. "And you should come with me to my aunt and uncle's ranch. It's just a few miles north of town."

"Everybody in the county knows where the Blue Spruce is." Lily glanced at her mother. "I think my mom and I should stick together."

"No one's after your mom," Nate said. "She'd be safer away from you."

"Oh." Lily and her mom looked at each other. Kate was still walking around wrapped in her afghan. She was pale and looked as if she'd rather be lying down.

"The man we arrested might sing like a canary when he gets to booking," Nate said. "Maybe he'll tell us his real name and who he works for and everything will be wrapped up tomorrow."

"That would be great," Lily muttered.

He wanted to take the frightened look from her eyes. But in all practicality, it was too soon. For tonight, at least, he wanted her worried enough that she'd let him take care of her.

"It's also possible he'll keep his mouth shut. And that the gunman who escaped will find you again."

Lily picked up one of the little mosquito dogs. "I have a couple of other part-time jobs here in town. I can't stay all the way out there on that ranch."

Her *life* was in danger and she was worried about some part-time jobs?

Nate knew she was an intelligent woman. But he could also see she was exhausted and not thinking straight.

"How about you go with me tonight. That way your mom can rest easier at Penny's house." He glanced at Kate, hoping she'd back him up. "You can rethink things tomorrow."

After a slight coughing fit, Lily's mom voiced her agreement.

Lily pursed her lips and blew out a sad, tired sigh while the dog she was holding sniffed her hair. "All right."

FOUR

Lily cracked open the window of Nate's truck and let the cold, sharp air swirl in and nip at her skin. Late autumn would be turning into early winter sometime before morning, she could feel it.

She looked into the darkness as the truck rolled down the highway, her thoughts turning bleaker with every mile. Her plan to get back on her feet after returning to her hometown had already been built on shaky ground, and now *this*. Her bank account wasn't going to get any healthier if she had to waste her time hiding out from criminals. It would take forever to pay down her bills and move out of her mother's house.

She glanced at Nate, wondering what his life had been like the last few years. He hadn't mentioned a wife, but that didn't mean he wasn't involved with someone. Not that it mattered. She just wondered.

He constantly checked the mirrors as he drove, watching to see if anyone was following them. Lily checked the mirrors, too. They still didn't know how those thugs had found her at her mother's house. They might have simply followed them from the Starlight Mart. But maybe they had access to her personal infor-

mation through someone at work. She sat up straighter
and put a little more energy into scanning for headlights behind them.

The narrow road they were traveling on was barely
more than a line of crumbling asphalt, and they continued to climb to a higher elevation. Most of the time,
tall pines lined the road, but every now and then there
was a break and she could see the glittering lights of
Copper Mesa down below.

"Can we turn on some music?" The tension and terror she'd felt over the last few hours had given her a
pounding headache.

"Music's not a good idea right now."

"Why not?"

He didn't really think he could *hear* someone following them over the rattling and squeaking sounds his old
truck made, did he? "It might be nice," she suggested
again, attempting to sound polite even though she was
speaking through gritted teeth. He didn't deserve her
wrath, but she couldn't help it. *She* didn't deserve to get
attacked—twice—and she wanted to punch somebody.
"I think it would help me relax."

"Well, then definitely no music. This isn't a good
time for you to relax. You need to stay sharp."

She didn't *want* to stay sharp. She wanted to go back
to taking her life for granted.

"What kind of lawman are you?" she demanded.
"Don't you know it's your job to make me feel safe?"
She turned to glare at him. In the amber glow from
the dashboard she saw the outline of his strong profile,
despite the beard. The warm light softened the lines
that time and Arizona sunlight had etched around his

eyes and he didn't look nearly as harsh as he had in the Starlight Mart.

"Are you absolutely certain you never saw either of those two thugs before? Hanging around work or maybe somewhere else?"

Lily looked out the window. How many times would he ask her that? Didn't he believe her?

"You heard me tell my story to the authorities. Twice." Lily turned toward him and tucked the hair that had fallen loose from her ponytail back behind her ear. He might be trying to help her, but she was tired of being interrogated. She hadn't done anything wrong. "Why do you keep asking me?"

"Sometimes it takes people a while to remember things." His tone was neutral, almost to the point of sounding cold. He'd started to feel like a friend as the evening wore on, but now he was slipping back into cop mode and she was stung by the realization he was still suspicious of her.

"How could you possibly think I've got some kind of connection with those two idiots?"

He glanced over at her. "People get dragged into situations and do things they didn't mean to. Or they agree to do something just once, because they're desperate, and before they know it they're in over their head."

"Yeah, well, *some* people are minding their own business when the next thing they know some jerk is trying to kill them." If he kept up these calm insinuations she just might jump out of the truck and walk the rest of the way to the ranch.

He loosened his grip on the steering wheel and leaned back a little. "If you're in some kind of trouble, I want you to know you can tell me. I'll help you."

"Oh, please. If you really believe I'm part of some criminal enterprise, why are you taking me to your aunt and uncle's ranch?"

He hesitated a few seconds before answering. "They're used to people with issues."

People with issues? Okay, that was it. She turned so she was rigidly facing forward. "Take me back to town. I can find someplace safe to stay on my own."

"Oh, lighten up. Everybody's got issues." He glanced over at her, this time with a slight smile that made her want to punch him. But he looked rock-solid and she'd probably just hurt her fist. "I've made some bad decisions in my life," he added, sounding a little more serious. "Needed help getting straightened out."

"Well, I don't have time to make any bad decisions. I work three jobs and sleep, and that's about it."

"Sounds exhausting. How long have you been doing that?"

Was he asking as a friend, or was he still in cop mode and fishing for information he could pass along to Sheriff Wolfsinger? Oh, she might as well tell him everything. It would come out sooner or later.

The truck hit a rut and bounced, and the springs squeaked.

After the truck settled, Lily took a deep breath. "I went to college in Flagstaff." She hesitated, trying to think of the moment when her life started to unravel.

"What did you get your degree in?" he prompted.

"I didn't finish my degree."

"What were you majoring in?"

"Accounting."

"So you like working with numbers?"

"No. But I thought the degree would help me earn a good living."

"That kind of thinking hardly ever works out."

"Yeah…well." It was tempting to let him think bad grades were the only issue. It was less humiliating than the truth.

"I didn't date much in high school or after," she said flatly. "I was too busy." And not burdened with an abundance of social skills. She turned her attention to the seat belt stretched across her shoulder and picked at a frayed thread. "I met someone in college. Kevin."

It was so easy now to see how stupid she'd been. Why hadn't she seen it then?

"We dated. We got engaged. My mind was on him instead of my studies. Then my thoughts were focused on our wedding, where we'd live, how I wanted to decorate our first home." She shook her head. "Stupid, stupid stuff." It was a dream come true. And at the end, as with a dream, there was nothing of substance left.

She was grateful Nate didn't say anything.

"I started working to earn money to help pay for everything. My grades suffered. I quit college. I told myself I'd go back after I got married and my life settled down. A few weeks later Kevin broke up with me. He'd found someone else."

She'd been heartbroken and bitterly disappointed in herself. Eventually she realized she'd been trying to create an oasis of certainty in her life when she got engaged to Kevin. Being away from home was scary. *Life* was scary. But a plan like that could never work.

"The guy was an idiot," Nate said.

Lily smiled. It was the perfect guy-friend thing to say. Not a suspicious-cop comment.

"I had to move back in with my mom in Copper Mesa. I've been working three part-time jobs. Torrent Trucking seemed like my best chance to move upward, maybe get on full-time. I thought if I got there a little early, stayed a little late and did a little extra work, my efforts might pay off."

And look where that had gotten her. Nearly killed. Twice.

Nate turned onto a narrow, unpaved road. The tires rumbled as the truck crossed a cattle guard. Shortly after that, he turned again. They passed by two sandstone pillars inset with bronze plaques identifying this as the Blue Spruce Ranch, and headed up a winding drive to the main house.

"So, am I still a suspect or do you finally believe my story?"

He glanced at her and then turned back to face the road. "I believe you."

"Good."

Lily had never seen the Blue Spruce Ranch in person, but she'd seen plenty of pictures. Ellen Stuart had inherited it from her parents and she was the fifth generation of Stuarts to run the land. Her marriage to Nate's uncle Bud, a "nobody" in county social circles, had caused quite a stir. They'd never had biological children of their own, but they'd opened their ranch to friends and various charity group events and created their own version of a family.

Nate drove along the wide, graceful driveway that followed the edge of a grassy field until the house came into view. It was a long, low ranch house with a covered porch running along the front of it. Lights blazed inside even though it was close to midnight. Nate pulled the truck around the circular drive and stopped. The front door flew open and Lily saw the silhouette of a short, round, bowlegged man with a bald head.

Nate came around and opened the door for her, a surprising bit of chivalry from a deputy just doing his job.

"Welcome to the Blue Spruce," Bud Wells called out to Lily. He walked up to her, reached for her hands and gave them a reassuring squeeze. "I'm Nate's uncle Bud. He told us what happened to you tonight and I'm as sorry as I can be about that."

"Lily Doyle." Lily barely trusted herself to speak. For the last few hours she'd held fear and dread at bay by indulging in frustration and denial. Being annoyed with Nate had helped. But now the gentle concern in Bud Wells's voice threatened to knock down a few bricks in the emotional wall she'd built and she couldn't let that happen. Not yet. The wall was the only thing keeping her from falling completely apart.

"Thank you for letting me come up here," she finally said.

Bud gave her hands another gentle squeeze before letting go of them. The compassionate expression in his eyes hardened into determination. "It's a rough world, Ms. Doyle, but you're safe here. And you're welcome to stay as long as you like."

"I appreciate that."

Bud glanced over at Nate. "Come here, boy."

Nate dutifully stepped up to the man who was noticeably shorter than him and bent down to give his uncle a hug. Bud wrapped his arms around his nephew's waist, and squeezed hard. "I worry about you every day, boy." Bud's face was pressed into Nate's shoulder and his voice was muffled, but Lily heard him. "I know better, but I can't help it."

He finally let go and took a step back. "All right, let's get in the house. Ellen's waiting for the both of you."

Lily stepped through the front door to a tiled foyer and the wide expanse of a great room with a fire burning low in a stone fireplace. To the right the room opened onto a dining area that curved around, presumably toward a kitchen.

A woman walked out from the kitchen area. Tall and slender, dressed in jeans and a raw silk blouse, she wore her long silver hair clipped back at the sides with turquoise barrettes. Ellen Wells. Responsible landowner. Astute businesswoman and, according to everything Lily had heard and read, the heartbeat of the sprawling Blue Spruce Ranch.

"Oh, honey, are you all right?" she asked Lily. Without waiting for an answer she walked up to Lily and hugged her as if she was a cherished friend and not a complete stranger. For a few seconds Lily let herself soak up the warmth of the embrace. Tears began to form in her eyes and she rapidly blinked them away. There were still good people in the world. Now more than ever she needed a reminder of that.

"I'm fine, thank you," Lily muttered as she stepped back.

"I'm sure the sheriff's department will find those men who came after you. In the meantime, we're always happy to have company."

Ellen smiled at her and Lily tried to smile back, but couldn't.

"You'll be all right," Ellen said softly. Then she turned to Nate, fisted her hands on her hips and looked him over from head to toe. "Well, you went downhill in a hurry."

Nate raked his fingers through his scruffy hair and scraggly beard. "What, you don't like the look?"

In an instant, Ellen had her arms around him in a hug. When she finally let go, she ran her hands up and down his arms a couple of times. "How about you? Are *you* all right?"

"Yes, ma'am."

A dark-haired man walked out from the kitchen and glanced at Nate.

"You look even uglier than usual," he said. He appeared to be about Nate's age, but he was a little shorter and slenderer with brown eyes and jet-black hair.

"I've intentionally been trying to look like a lowlife for the last six weeks," Nate shot back. "What's your excuse?"

The dark-haired man grinned. "Welcome home. I'm glad you didn't get yourself killed."

Ellen threw up her hands. "Don't talk like that!"

The man walked over to give Nate a one-armed embrace and clapped him on the shoulder.

Lily caught Bud giving both men a cautioning look. Then he turned to her. "Lily, this is Gaston Juneau. He moved up here about the time Nate did when they were kids. Works as a foreman here when he isn't out in the wilderness trying to make Ellen grayer and me balder by fighting wildfires."

Gaston nodded. "Good to meet you. Nobody's going to bother you while you're up here. We'll make sure of that."

A thump and a squeak made Lily turn around. An empty upholstered chair rocked back and forth in front of the fireplace. A few seconds later an enormous orange-and-white cat sauntered around the chair.

"Hank!" Nate picked up the cat and hefted him into the crook of his arm. The cat put his paws on Nate's shoulder and head-butted him.

Ellen chuckled. "We've all been missing you. Hank included." She turned to Lily. "What can I get you to eat?"

"Thank you, but I'm not hungry. I'd really just like to get some rest."

Ellen looked at her thoughtfully. "I know you're exhausted. Did you bring a suitcase?"

Lily nodded.

Ellen turned to her husband. "Honey, would you get Lily's bag out of Nate's truck?"

"Sure." Bud headed for the front door.

"Your room is this way," Ellen said, heading down a hallway.

Behind her, Lily heard Gaston say to Nate, "Get some sleep. I'll keep watch until morning."

Ellen led her to a beautiful room with an attached bath. Bud delivered her bag and both he and Ellen wished her a good night.

After they left, Lily kicked off her shoes, pulled down the top blanket and let herself fall face-first onto the bed. Eventually she pulled up the blanket, but left the bedside lamp on. A Bible lay on the nightstand. It had been a while since she'd picked one up, but looking at it made her feel a little calmer. If she couldn't sleep, maybe she'd read a few verses.

It was good to know Nate was nearby. But as cozy and secure as this house felt, she was still in danger. And because of her, everyone else at the Blue Spruce was in danger, too.

* * *

"Now you don't look like a deadbeat anymore." Bud grabbed a towel and slapped at Nate's shoulders and the back of his neck while Nate sat in an old straight-backed chair. They were outside, at the far end of the rambling front porch.

Nate rubbed his hand over his head to feel the familiar short bristle cut, then over his smooth chin and cheeks. He'd shaved off his whiskers right after he'd rolled out of bed this morning. "That feels a lot better."

"Nothing wrong with looking sharp for your lady friend."

Nate turned to glare at his uncle and Bud winked at him.

"I just wanted to get the grime from working under-cover off of me," Nate said. "I had to be around some nasty people in some filthy places." That was the truth. Maybe it was also true he wanted to look a little cleaner for Lily Doyle, too. Let her see that he'd made something of his life and hadn't hit the skids like his mom had. Like so many people assumed he would.

"Well, you're home and away from those terrible places now, boy." Bud shook the towel over the railing and Nate stood up.

When Nate had first woken up, the trees and the rooftops of the ranch buildings had all been covered in a hard freeze. Things had warmed up a little since then, but the air still carried a cold edge to it.

It was beautiful here no matter the weather. There were plenty of mornings when he woke up in his apartment in Painted Rock and missed being able to spend a few minutes sipping coffee and looking at this view of pine trees, mountain meadows and rocky peaks. But he'd done what he thought was right. Somebody had to make sure the people who'd been responsible for his mother's death faced justice. And if getting exiled to Painted Rock was the price he had to pay, so be it.

It hadn't been revenge, despite loud accusations to the contrary. He knew vengeance didn't belong to him.

He'd had the opportunity to take down a trio of drug dealers and he'd jumped at it. They'd hired a sharp defense lawyer out of Phoenix who decided his best tactic was to ignore his clients' blatant drug trafficking and smear the Oso County sheriff's department, instead. Fortunately, the lawyer hadn't been successful in keeping his clients out of prison. But during the trial he had managed to turn the trustworthiness of the sheriff's department into the hotly debated topic of the day. Sheriff Wolfsinger could have buckled under the political pressure and fired Nate. He transferred him to Painted Rock instead.

"So, you knew Lily in high school?" Bud asked as he folded up his towel. "I don't remember her."

Good old Uncle Bud, gamely trying to engage Nate in a conversation. It wasn't always easy for Nate to talk about how he was feeling. He'd spent a long time as a kid trying not to feel anything.

He glanced at his uncle. Sometimes Nate forgot he wasn't the only one who was abandoned when his mom dove into the emotionally numbing abyss of alcohol and later, in a fatal decision, into drugs. Uncle Bud had lost his sister, too.

"I didn't know Lily," Nate said, trying to lighten his tone. "Joseph Suh did."

"Oh. Well, Ellen's glad to see you brought a girl home." Nate laughed and shook his head. "This isn't a date."

His smile faded. "I was hoping she'd just need a safe place to stay for one night. But I called the station this morning and I think we're going to need to find her a place to stay for a little longer." The news he'd gotten from Sheriff Wolfsinger when he'd called asking for an update was not good.

"We've got plenty of room here. You know she's welcome."

"I appreciate that."

Nate heard a meow. A few seconds later Hank wandered around the side of the house and stepped up onto the porch, shaking the dampness of melted frost from his front paws. The cat sat down and his rather large body compacted into the shape of a ball. He rolled slightly to one side.

"Your cat's getting too fat," Bud said.

"I'm not the one who's been feeding him lately. I've been in Phoenix, remember?" Nate stood, picked up the cat and hefted him into the crook of his arm. He turned toward the front door to head back into the house. "Thanks for the haircut."

Bud dropped the scissors he'd been using to cut Nate's hair into a leather shaving kit. "You're welcome."

In the kitchen, Ellen had taken a breakfast casserole out of the oven and was scooping a mixture of hash browns, eggs, sausage and cheese onto heavy ceramic plates on the counter. It smelled wonderful, and Gaston hovered nearby, obviously ready to eat.

Nate glanced at Lily, surprised to see that she was up this early. It would take Nate a few more days to shake off the adrenaline and hypervigilance resulting from his assignment down in Phoenix, but last night Lily had looked tired enough to sleep until noon.

"Good morning." He felt self-conscious because she was staring at him so intently. Maybe she was wondering why she'd let him bring her up here.

"You cut your hair and shaved," she said.

"Oh. Yeah." She was still watching him and Nate figured it was his turn to say something, but he couldn't think of a response.

Gaston, who'd stayed up all night and hadn't gone to bed yet, leaned toward Lily. "Do you think he looked better with his face all covered up?"

"No. I, uh…" She took a sip of coffee without finishing her answer.

"I called Sheriff Wolfsinger and got an update," Nate said. "Do you want to hear it now, or after we've eaten?"

Lily gripped her coffee mug with both hands and took a deep breath. "Tell me now."

"We've got an ID on the loser we caught last night. The one in the hoodie. His name's Jack Covert."

"Well, that's good. That's something."

"Yeah, but he's not talking. He's got a lengthy criminal history and ties to organized crime. Specifically to a criminal group the task force suspects is involved in the multistate cargo thefts."

When her eyes widened, he knew she'd realized the seriousness of what he was telling her.

"Yeah," he said. "It's just as we suspected. What you heard, or what they *think* you heard, could potentially bring down a multimillion-dollar theft ring. Instead of things blowing over fairly quickly, they're likely to get a whole lot worse."

FIVE

"It feels odd to see the parking lot nearly empty on a weekday," Lily said.

Nate glanced over at her. She'd been subdued since he'd told her about the established connection between organized crime and at least one of the people who'd tried to kill her. She hadn't eaten much breakfast. She'd just quietly sipped coffee until it was time to drive to Torrent Trucking for her purse and her phone, and then on to the Starlight Mart for her car.

Nate pulled his truck into the expansive oiled-dirt parking lot of Torrent Trucking. Bryan Torrent was the single owner of the thirty-acre plot of land near the crossroads twenty miles from Copper Mesa, where there was plenty of room for semi drivers to maneuver without having to contend with traffic in town. The warehouse-and-office complex stood at the end of a short private road just off the highway.

"You all right?" Nate asked Lily. "I can take you back to the ranch and bring your purse and phone to you later. Your car will be fine at the Starlight Mart for a few more days."

She shook her head. "I want to be here. I need to know what's going on."

"Okay." It was the same sentiment she'd expressed when he'd tried to talk her into staying up at the ranch and letting him figure out a way to fetch her belongings without her.

She pointed to an office door facing the road. "That's where I work. I left my purse and phone in there."

He parked near the door and cut the engine. Sheriff Wolfsinger pulled his patrol car into the parking lot a few seconds later. Nate and Lily got out of the truck and met up with him.

"I just got off the phone with Bryan Torrent," Wolfsinger said after a quick exchange of greetings. "He should be here in a few minutes. Claims he's on his way home from the airport after a business trip to Los Angeles."

"Did he say anything else?" Nate asked.

"Just that he'd heard about what happened to Lily. Said he was horrified something like that could happen to one of his employees."

"He doesn't know much about the specifics, right?"

Wolfsinger shook his head. "And we're going to limit what we tell him. Our bad guy in custody still hasn't given us any useful information. I want to get a read on Mr. Torrent before we share any details."

They walked up to the office door, where they were met by a solidly built man around Nate's age with red hair, gelled and combed straight back.

"Hey, Lily. What a relief to see you're okay." The red-haired man moved toward her as if he was going to hug her. She stepped back.

"Thanks, Eddie." She turned to Nate. "This is Eddie

Drake. He's the evening warehouse supervisor." Nate gave him a nod and Sheriff Wolfsinger stepped up to introduce himself. Nate watched Eddie steal glances at Lily during the course of their introductory chit-chat. She remained well away from him with her arms crossed.

They walked inside the building and stood in a small reception area that had a couple of desks, chairs and some storage cabinets. Through an open door in the back Nate could see a hallway leading farther into the building.

"Do you usually work overnight and into the morning?" Sheriff Wolfsinger asked Eddie.

"Nope. Normally my hours are noon to nine. I'm just here this morning because Mr. Torrent called and asked me to come in."

"What did he say when he called?" Wolfsinger asked.

"That he'd heard what had happened to Lily." He glanced in her direction.

The high school kids who'd been in the Starlight Mart had been all over social media telling of their experience. Local news media had picked up the story so everybody in town had a general idea of what had happened.

"He told me to shut everything down and send everybody home. He said to reroute all the deliveries scheduled to come through the facility for the next three days. One of our dispatchers, Sheila, is over in the dispatch room making sure it's all been taken care of."

"Did he say why he wanted to do that?"

Nate was curious, too.

Eddie shrugged. "He told me he'd meant to update security around here for a while. He's getting new keycard locks for all the doors before everyone returns to work and putting in a system to track the identity of anyone who comes into our buildings. He wants to put up some fencing around the property, maybe even hire a twenty-four-hour security-guard service."

Nate glanced at Wolfsinger. It could be the reaction of a business owner shocked to learn his employee had nearly been murdered. But it might be a sign that Torrent knew about the larger criminal connection to what had happened to Lily and he was worried. Maybe he was even involved in it.

"Is there any surveillance footage of the property available?" Nate asked.

"Afraid not," Eddie answered. "There are video cameras in place, but the system's so old it's fallen apart and we've never updated it."

Wolfsinger glanced toward the door that opened onto the hallway. "Could I speak to your dispatcher?"

"Sure." Eddie stepped through the door and called out, "Sheila, can you come in here?"

A few seconds later a young blonde woman in jeans and a flowery sweater strolled into the front office. She was chewing gum and smiling broadly until she saw who was in the room. Then she stopped chewing and her smile vanished. Nate couldn't tell if her good mood was deflated by the sight of Sheriff Wolfsinger, or the sight of Lily.

Eddie made the introductions.

"I don't want to take up too much of your time," Sheriff Wolfsinger said. "But I'd like to know if you've seen or heard anything that might help us understand what happened to Ms. Doyle."

Sheila turned to Lily and cocked her head to the side.

"I'm so sorry about what happened to you, but I don't know anything." Then she glanced at Nate and gave him a slight smile.

"Have any new drivers you've never worked with before come through here in the last few days?"

"They might have. I really couldn't tell you for sure. It's hard to keep track of everybody who passes through here."

"Understandable." Wolfsinger offered her a patient smile. "Have you seen anybody new back in your break room?"

"I usually eat lunch at my desk."

"Okay." He handed her his card. "If you think of something later, give me a call."

"Sure." She glanced around the room, her gaze snagging on Eddie for a few lingering seconds before she left.

"I want to do everything I can to catch the guys who did this to you." Eddie gave Lily an encouraging smile as soon as the dispatcher was out of the room.

Nate was curious to see Lily's reaction. She nodded once, a bare-bones acknowledgment. Then she headed over to a desk and picked up the cell phone and purse that were sitting on top of it.

"Mr. Drake, who would have paperwork showing who came through here over the last few days?" Sheriff Wolfsinger asked the warehouse supervisor.

"You're talking about drivers?"

The sheriff nodded.

"Should be in the computer system," Lily interjected, walking back toward them.

Eddie glanced at her, then looked past her at something outside a window. Nate followed his gaze and watched as a metallic gold luxury sedan pulled into the parking lot and stopped just outside the entrance. "I think Mr. Torrent might want to have a say in who goes through company computer records," Eddie said cautiously. "That's him right there."

A tall, slender man, wearing a sharply tailored gray suit, climbed out of the car. His dark hair fell into place with the studied casualness of an expensive cut. He walked through the door and greeted the sheriff.

"Thank you for meeting us here," Wolfsinger responded. "This is Deputy Nate Bedford."

"Glad to meet you." Torrent extended his hand and Nate shook it.

"And I'm sure you know your employee, Lily Doyle," the sheriff added.

"Actually, we've never met. We hired Lily through an employment service." Torrent strode toward her and extended his hand. "It's terrible what happened to you. Is there anything you need?"

"I'm fine."

"I understand you haven't been working for us for very long, but that you've done an excellent job while you've been here. Please, take a couple of weeks off. I'll pay you for them. And when you're ready to come back, I think we can use you full-time. And give you a raise."

She smiled at him. "Thank you."

Nate thought Torrent held Lily's hand a little longer than he needed to before he finally let it go.

"You must have heard about the trailer and cargo thefts along the highways that pass through the area," Wolfsinger said. "You haven't reported anything stolen. Have you had any trouble with theft?"

"Cargo theft?" Torrent raised his eyebrows and then

shook his head. "No, I haven't." He glanced at Lily. "What has that got to do with what happened to Lily?"

"It's an ongoing investigation," Wolfsinger replied, smoothly deflecting his question. "Are you aware the two men who took over the Starlight Mart had been seen here at your facility earlier in the day?"

Torrent drew his head back in surprise. "They were my employees?"

"Or drivers passing through and making use of your break room."

His expression turned into a scowl and his face flushed with anger. "I'll send you digital copies of the drivers' manifests immediately. Eddie, how do we access that information?" He glanced back at Wolfsinger. "I don't spend much time here."

Eddie sat at a computer, asked the sheriff for his email address, and a couple of minutes later Wolfsinger's phone chimed. The sheriff glanced down at the screen. "Got it."

"That's everything for the last thirty days," Eddie said. He moved his mouse to scroll through the images on his computer. "Looks like it's all been regular drivers passing through."

"This will help us dig into things a little deeper." The sheriff looked up from his phone. "Thank you for your time." He gestured to Nate that it was time to go.

Lily started to walk out the door and Eddie stepped in front of her. Nate's muscles tightened and irritation shot through his body like a zap of electric current. If Lily wanted Eddie moved out of her way, Nate would be happy to move him. Because it was his job. As a lawman. And he was nothing but professional.

"I hope this terrible incident doesn't scare you away,"

Eddie said to Lily with a toothy, hopeful smile. "You are returning to work when things get back to normal, right?"

She glanced at Bryan Torrent, who was now sitting on the edge of a desk, still fuming. Torrent saw her looking at him, relaxed his expression slightly and managed a faint, encouraging smile.

Lily responded with a weak smile of her own. "I think I'll be back."

Eddie moved out of her way.

"Before all of this happened, had you seen or heard anything unusual going on around here?" Nate asked Lily after they were outside and well away from Torrent and Eddie.

"I couldn't tell you. I haven't been working here long enough to know what's unusual."

Wolfsinger had taken a few steps away from them with his phone to his ear. He disconnected from a call and walked back toward them.

"Nate, I know if I tell you to butt out of this investigation and head back to the Blue Spruce to relax you probably won't listen to me. And the fact is you're going to be back on duty in a week, anyway, so you might as well stay up to speed."

"Appreciate it."

"You're still assigned to Painted Rock even while you're working on the task force. That's not changing. It might be a small town in the middle of nowhere, but they get big rig traffic cutting across the mountain pass up there. It's possible the cargo thieves are breaking down their goods into less noticeable amounts and hauling them across the back roads."

"I'll keep an eye out for that as soon as I get back on duty."

Wolfsinger glanced around at the empty parking lot where they stood and sighed. "I don't like this. The attempted hits on Lily look like pure panic. Whoever's behind them will want to finish the job and tie up any loose ends. After you pick up Lily's car, you both better stay out of sight for a while."

"We'll head right back to the ranch."

"Good. I just got off the phone with Deputy Rios. She and Bubba will meet you at the Starlight Mart to make sure Lily's car is safe to move and hasn't been rigged with explosives."

"Explosives?" Lily's eyes widened.

"There's big money involved here," Wolfsinger said to her. "And somebody thinks you've gotten in their way." His phone started to ring. He answered it and turned away, heading toward his patrol car.

Nate opened the passenger door of his truck for Lily, then walked around and got in. He started up the engine.

"Rios and Bubba?" Lily asked, her voice a little shaky.

"They'll make sure nothing bad happens to you."

"Deputy *Bubba*?" Lily muttered. "That's got to be a nickname."

"I don't know his legal name," Nate said. "But he's very good at what he does."

Lily gazed through the dusty front windshield of Nate's truck. They'd reached the intersection with the highway that ran north toward Painted Rock. There, perched on a corner, was the Starlight Mart. The owner didn't put much effort into maintaining the store's appearance. He didn't have to. If you were this far out of Copper Mesa and low on fuel, craving a microwave burrito or dying for a sugary drink, you'd stop. There was nowhere else to go.

The Starlight Mart was Lily's only option last night and she was fortunate the dilapidated old store was here. If those two thugs had caught her on the highway, or if her car had run out of gas in the darkness… She shuddered at the thought and reminded herself she was all right. *Thank You, Lord.*

Nate made the bumpy turn off the highway into the store parking lot. Lily spotted her secondhand olive-green sedan right where she'd left it last night.

An Oso County sheriff's department patrol car was parked by the side of the store and Nate pulled up next to it. The car door opened and a deputy got out. She opened the back door of her car and a large black-and-tan police dog hopped down.

"How ya doing?" the deputy called out to them as the dog sat obediently at her feet. The deputy's jet-black hair was pulled back in a French braid with a sweep of bangs. Dark glasses hid her eyes. She wore a thick jacket for protection against the cold breeze.

"I'm doing all right," Nate answered as he and Lily climbed out of his truck. "Crystal, this is Lily Doyle. Lily, meet Deputy Crystal Rios. She's covering my territory up around Painted Rock until I officially return from leave. And that's her partner, Bubba."

Lily nodded a greeting at the deputy, then turned to the handsome dog, who looked at her with intelligent, coffee-colored eyes. "He's a beauty."

"He is," Rios agreed. "And right now he's going to work." She gave a command and Bubba got to his feet.

They started toward Lily's parked car. Rios led Bubba around the car, giving him encouragement and directions as the K-9 gave everything a good sniff.

"Bomb detection is one of Bubba's many skills," Nate said. "He's an excellent tracker, too."

Lily hugged herself. She was cold and a little freaked out. "Do you really believe my car needs to be checked out for some kind of bomb?"

"Plenty of people will do anything for money," Nate said, watching Rios and Bubba at work. "Theft of cargo along the interstate is big business. We're talking tens of millions of dollars in a single month. If someone believes you overheard something that could expose their plans, it would be worth a lot to get rid of you."

"I never thought about things getting stolen out here," Lily said, glancing at the highway. Cold facts were something she could handle right now. She steered the conversation in that direction. Dwelling on the potential danger to her was just a little too much.

"Electronics, tech equipment, phones, pharmaceuticals. You name it," Nate said. "Everything's got to be transported somehow. Small-time thieves break into parked trailers and grab the stuff inside. Organized criminals take the entire trailer."

Lily shivered. It wasn't just from the cold. She turned her attention back to Bubba as he sniffed around her car. Deputy Rios kept up a steady stream of direction and encouragement for her dog.

"I don't understand how the thieves can get away with it," Lily said. "The trailers have tracking components in them. For that matter, so do the tractors." She'd learned that working at Torrent Trucking.

"I don't have any inside information since I haven't

officially checked in with the task force yet," Nate said. "But I'd guess someone has figured out a way to disrupt the tracking system."

"Bubba is signaling we're clear," Deputy Rios called out.

Nate and Lily walked toward her.

After lavishly praising Bubba and giving him a drink of water, Deputy Rios let him into the backseat of her patrol car and tossed him a squeaky toy. He caught it and chewed happily as she shut the door.

"Do you need us for anything else?" she asked Nate.

"Nope."

"Okay." She got into her patrol car and started the engine. "Be careful," she called out, and then she drove off.

"Let me see your keys," Nate said.

Lily dug them out of her pocket. He took them, got into her car and started the engine. Then he drove the few feet over to one of the pumps and started filling the tank with gas.

"Let me take care of this and we'll head back up to the ranch," Nate said as she walked up to him.

"I'll be up there as soon as I talk to my bosses for my two other jobs."

Nate raised his eyebrows, looking at her as if she was out of her mind.

"I need to tell them in person what happened and ask for a couple of days off. To show them I'm not some flaky new employee making up a wild story because I don't want to come into work."

"But Bryan Torrent offered you a full-time job. Aren't you going to take it?"

"Probably. But I want to keep my options open." She

sighed. "It felt creepy being back there and I'm not sure I could go back every day without thinking about what happened. But I really need the money."

"So what's going on between you and Eddie Drake?"

"Nothing. I work with him. That's it." She crossed her arms over her chest and felt her eyes narrow. "You're just dying to find some dirt on me, aren't you? Why?"

"I know what I saw." He ignored her questions and leaned against her car. A taunting smile played across his lips while the gas pump kept running. "I'm a trained observer. There's something between you two."

He kept his tone light, but it was clear he expected an answer.

She turned away and looked at the neon signs in the Starlight Mart window. For a moment it felt like she was back in there, terrified and on the verge of hopelessness. She tried to shake off the feeling and turned back to Nate. He'd saved her life when he walked in there. She owed him. "Eddie talks about himself a lot. Trying to impress me, I think. And he's asked me out a few times."

"But you turned him down?"

"I'm not interested." She took a deep breath. "The last thing I want to do is get involved with anyone. I have a life to rebuild."

"I understand. Not everybody is looking for a date. I'm not exactly husband material myself. Obviously."

Not husband material? What did *that* mean? No, wait. She wasn't going to let herself even start to wonder about that. It didn't matter.

"Look, I'm not especially brave," she said, turning the conversation back toward her objective goals. "I want to hide as soon as I can and stay hidden until somebody can figure out what's going on. But while I'm in town I need to make sure my mom's okay. Then I need to stop at a couple of places and talk to my bosses. I'll make it quick, I promise. And I'll see you back at the Blue Spruce in an hour."

"You'll see me in your rearview mirror."

Her heart fluttered and she didn't want it to. She needed to stay practical, not get all loopy over an acquaintance who was probably helping her because he wanted to honor an old friend. It wasn't personal. He was obviously trying to remind her of that with the husband-material comment.

"Don't they need your help at the ranch?" she asked, grasping for a reason to send him on his way.

"Gaston won't have anything to complain about if I start helping him on my first day back. He'll hate that." Nate took the nozzle out of the car, attached it back to the pump and snapped the gas cap shut. "Look, I know you want to get back to normal life as soon as you can. But the gunman who got away last night is still out there. He knows where you live. He knows what your car looks like. He's probably hanging around watching and waiting for his chance to get to you."

Lily started to feel as if the wintry air brushing the surface of her skin had sunk down into her bones.

"It's too dangerous for you to go into town alone," Nate said. "So I'm going with you."

SIX

"I'll see you again soon, girls." Lily stood in Penny's living room and held the mini dachshunds, Abby and Beatrice, in her arms. She gave each one a light squeeze and a kiss on the head. Beatrice squirmed and tried to return the kiss while Abby gave Lily the stoic look of a dog who'd been betrayed.

"I *will* see you soon," she repeated to Abby before setting both dogs on the ground. Beatrice ran over to Lily's mom, who claimed she was feeling better even though she was still coughing as badly as she had been last night. Abby remained by Lily's feet and stared at Nate as if she thought he might steal the kibble.

They'd left Lily's car parked on a side street near the sheriff's department rather than taking it back to the house, where someone might be watching for Lily. Nate had insisted on driving it, just to be safe. Lily had driven his truck. After they'd dropped off the car, Lily had promised Nate she'd keep the visit with her mom short. They'd already been there fifteen minutes, so she hugged Kate and Penny, reassured them, said goodbye and headed for the front door. "I'll phone you in the morning," she called out before yanking the door open.

"Wait." Nate's large hand grabbed her upper arm and held her in place. He stepped around her onto the porch and looked up and down the street. "Okay, let's go."

In the truck, Lily gave him directions to Cozy Kitchen Caterers. She worked there several hours a week making sandwiches and baked goods. She had the most fun at that job and she really wanted to keep it.

"Have you been able to remember anything more about what you overheard?" Nate asked after they'd driven for a while. They stopped at a light and he glanced over at her. She could tell by his eyes that he was back in full cop mode. She wondered if it was even a conscious decision. Maybe when you grew up like he did you learned to always weigh and measure what people said and never assume they were telling you the truth.

"I heard the random words I already told you about. They were enough to alarm me, but not specific enough to get anybody busted for anything." If those two idiots had any sense, they would have claimed they were just talking about a movie. She would have believed them. "I definitely didn't hear anything worth going through all this trouble to try and kill me."

She paused and cleared her throat. People were trying to *kill* her. She could make it all seem matter-of-fact when she thought about it, but saying it aloud made her feel shaky and her voice wavered. "You already have one of the guys in custody. Can't you learn what you need to know by checking his background?"

"That probably won't be enough." They stopped at a traffic light and waited until it turned green. "What about your former fiancé? Could all of this be some sort of elaborate setup? An attempt at revenge?"

Lily winced just thinking about Kevin and all the stupid decisions she'd made from the first day she'd met him. He was a jerk, but he wasn't a killer. And the foolish decisions had been completely her own. "Now you're being ridiculous."

"Just checking every angle. Tell me about him."

"My former fiancé is not a criminal," she said. "He's an assistant city planner for a small town near Phoenix. And remember, he dumped me. Not the other way around." And enough water had passed under the bridge for her to be truly grateful about that. She hadn't realized that until right this minute.

Nate glanced at the cross streets as he drove. "I don't like staying in town. I'd rather get you back to the ranch right now."

Lily sighed. He didn't get it. He thought she was foolish worrying about a couple of meaningless, low-paying jobs. It was about the money, but it wasn't *just* about the money. "My dad died when I was a kid, like yours did. Only my dad wasn't a military man. He was a businessman and he had a stroke."

She glanced at Nate for a reaction. He was looking ahead through the window, waiting for her to say whatever she had to say at her own pace.

"Anyway, my mom worked hard for years. I worked hard in school. I wanted to go to college, get a degree and be able to take care of my mom financially."

"So that's why you were so brainy." He had a slight smile on his lips.

"Hardly brainy. But I did the best I could. I didn't win much in the way of scholarship money so I worked for a while after high school, saved my money, went to community college and finally went away to the university."

She'd had such a good, sharp, focused plan when she'd left town.

"Bottom line," she said briskly. "I'm broke, back home and a burden to my mom. I can't let that go on. I *have* to have money coming in. I won't have my mom paying my way when I should be taking care of her." And she wouldn't stop the fight to regain her self-respect.

He sighed. "When we get to your workplaces we'll make it fast. We go in, you talk and we get out. Five minutes maximum, each stop."

"Deal."

"And while we're driving around, tell me again what you overheard. I know you're sick of rehashing it, but sometimes people remember a small detail that's important."

"All right." Lily made herself focus on those frightening moments that had set off the terrifying chain reaction of events. Her heart rate sped up as she remembered walking through the office and hearing the voices. "Early Wednesday. They were saying something about 'early Wednesday.'"

"Wednesday?" Nate asked. "Tomorrow? What about it and how early?"

She shook her head. "I don't know." She'd just now remembered hearing those words.

Nate pulled to the side of the road and made a quick call to Sheriff Wolfsinger. Lily could hear their conversation. The end result was that Wolfsinger would have some deputies watch Torrent Trucking starting tonight.

"You think Bryan Torrent might be involved in the truck hijackings?" Lily asked after Nate disconnected.

"He claims to be a hands-off owner and that matches

what you've seen. Maybe someone else is using his facilities and he doesn't know about it."

They reached the catering company and Lily's boss, horrified to hear what had happened to her, was very understanding about Lily's need to take a few days off. As they left, Lily felt her spirits rise. Maybe things really would be okay. "It's no coincidence that my bosses all started their own businesses," she told Nate as they got back into his truck. "I chose the jobs for that reason. I hope to learn something from them."

"You want to open your own business?"

"Maybe. My mom worked a collection of odd jobs for years, some of them as an independent saleswoman. I felt bad that she had to work so hard, but when I stop to think about it I realize she always seemed happy." Lily's plan to climb the corporate ladder had crashed and burned when she'd flunked out of college. She'd needed a new plan and opening her own business one day seemed to be a good option.

It was a short drive to Ruby's Plant and Pottery Shop. Perched on a steep hill just a few yards back from one of Copper Mesa's main roads, the front of the building was a glass-wrapped showroom.

They went inside and Lily found Ruby.

"If someone had pointed a gun at me last night, I'd be at home hiding under my bed right this very minute." Ruby patted Lily's shoulder. "You come back to work when you're ready."

"I appreciate that."

The door opened and Ruby excused herself to help the arriving customer.

"While we're here I want get a thank-you gift for Bud and Ellen."

Nate pointedly looked at his watch.

Ruby's husband, Scott, had been hovering nearby while Lily talked to Ruby. "We've got some pretty cool stuff that's just arrived," he said. "Let me show you."

He led her toward a side door. Behind her, Lily heard Nate answer his phone.

"Look," Scott said when they got outside. He pointed down. "Garden stepping stones shaped like paw prints. I've put some down on the grass here to show how they'd look."

The cold weather had left the grass looking faint, but the stepping stones were still cute.

"These are adorable," Lily said, having to raise her voice over the sound of traffic on the nearby road.

The traffic sounds grew even louder and she glanced toward the street. A car barreled up the driveway to the store. It was going too fast, and Lily realized in a burst of panic it was speeding up and heading straight for her and Scott. "Run!"

The car jumped the parking lot curb and plowed up the hillside. Lily scrambled to get out of the way, but slid on the grass and fell. Horrified, she watched as Scott tried to get out of the way, too, and the car knocked him down.

The driver kept going, wheeling the car directly toward Lily. She crawled away as fast as she could, trying desperately to get some traction on the slick grass so she could get up and run. At the last second she dropped and rolled out of the way. The car missed her, but the sharp edge of its cracked bumper sliced across her thigh.

Her leg felt as if it had been skewered by a red-hot poker. She fought to get to her feet but the searing pain made her head swim.

The driver tried to turn the car around, but got bogged down. He gunned the engine. The car stayed in place while the wheels smoked and squealed and dug into the dirt and tossed up grass.

The crazed driver finally let off the gas pedal.

Then he fired a shot through the open side window of his car, the bullet shattering the plate glass window of the plant shop just behind Lily.

Through the chaos she heard Nate yelling something, but couldn't make sense of his words.

The car door flung open and the gunman from the Starlight Mart, the one who'd later gotten away by running down into the ravine by her mother's house, got out of the car. Wild-eyed, he looked directly at Lily and raised his gun.

There was a cluster of trees on the store property and Lily ran for it, her thigh throbbing so painfully she nearly passed out. Despite the adrenaline coursing through her veins, she couldn't put much weight on her leg and she ended up not moving much faster than a walk.

"You're dead!" the man huffed out as he chased her. "You're finally dead."

She could hear him getting closer and she couldn't move any faster. Straining forward with every bit of strength she had, she was afraid to look back. Her injured leg started to buckle. From behind, grasping fingers reached out and clasped the back of her jacket, jerking her to a stop. She felt the bite of the tip of a gun barrel pressed against her neck. *Again.*

Terrified and angry, she tried to spin around. If he was going to shoot her, he'd have to look her in the eyes. But she couldn't spin around. Couldn't see him.

He had too tight of a grip on her jacket. She could, however, turn far enough to see the tall shadow of a large lawman.

"Nate!" His name came out sounding more like a whisper than the shout she'd intended.

Sirens wailed in the distance.

The gunman loosened his grip and now Lily could turn. She saw Nate with his weapon drawn. And she saw the gunman with his pistol pointed at her, just inches from her head. Still clinging to Lily's jacket, the gunman tried to drag her farther up the hill. She didn't make it easy for him. "Cops are here," she managed to say, fighting for her breath. "You won't get away again."

In a panic she flung out her arm, intent on getting that gun out of her face. To her surprise, she connected hard enough to send the weapon out of the man's hand and to the ground. She quickly slid her foot, knocking the weapon farther away. The gunman made a move as if to reach down for it, but then glanced past Lily's shoulder, shoved her to the ground, and turned and ran out of sight behind the storage trailer instead.

Strong hands wrapped around Lily's upper arms and pulled her to her feet. "You're hurt." Nate wrapped an arm around her shoulder, holding her up.

Lily looked down at her leg. Her jeans were torn along her thigh and the fabric was soaked in blood.

The sound of barking caught her attention and she looked up as Deputy Rios and Bubba hustled out of a patrol car. Two more patrol cars pulled up behind them. Nate gestured toward the area where the gunman had disappeared, but Bubba already had a bead on the bad guy and was anxious to go. Rios let him lead the way while she and the other deputies followed close behind.

Nate held Lily a little bit tighter.

"I'll survive," she said. She looked around. "What about Scott?"

She looked back toward the store where Ruby's husband lay on the ground, moaning. Ruby and a customer kneeled beside him. An ambulance pulled up and the EMTs rushed out and hurried toward him.

Back in the direction of the storage trailer, people were yelling and Bubba was barking. All the action was happening on the other side of the trailer and Lily couldn't see a thing.

She heard a single gunshot and her heart froze in fear. In an instant she heard more yelling and the sounds of a struggle. Then it all stopped.

She held her breath until a couple of deputies appeared around the storage trailer with the gunman in handcuffs. Deputy Rios and Bubba followed, the K-9 prancing with the pride of a job well done.

SEVEN

"Obviously the man was desperate." Deputy Rios folded her arms over her chest and leaned back against a wall. "That lunatic tried to kill Lily in broad daylight in front of multiple witnesses."

"I'm just grateful you and Bubba happened to be in town for a meeting when it happened instead of up in Painted Rock covering for Nate," Lily said quietly.

They were at the sheriff's department's headquarters in downtown Copper Mesa. Ben Wolfsinger's office was in a historic old stone-block building that had housed territorial prisoners over a century ago. A covered walkway connected it to the modern facility, where the bulk of law enforcement administration was carried out.

The worn redbrick floor was uneven and chipped from decades of use. As Nate impatiently paced from one end of the room to the other, he had to watch where he stepped to keep from losing his balance. He was grateful for the distraction. It kept him from staring at Lily.

The woman he'd promised to protect had nearly gotten killed right before his eyes. The EMTs had cleaned and taped up her injured leg and then Nate had driven her to the hospital, where an X-ray had confirmed nothing was broken. After receiving a couple of injections to ward off nasty infections, the deep cut in her thigh had been stitched up and she was released.

Scott, the co-owner of the shop, was not so fortunate. His condition had worsened and he was in the ICU at the hospital, completely unresponsive.

Lily felt guilty about Scott's injuries. She'd said so. Nate tried to get her to direct the blame for what had happened on the gunman, but she blamed herself for leading the gunman to the plant shop. Every time Nate looked at her and saw the haunted expression in her eyes behind those librarian-like glasses, he wanted to wrap his arms around her.

But comforting someone on such a deeply emotional level wasn't what a deputy sheriff was hired to do. Nate knew his boundaries. He *liked* his boundaries.

Lily sat in Wolfsinger's padded desk chair at the sheriff's insistence, her injured leg stretched out straight in front of her. She wore the navy blue sweatpants and sweatshirt Deputy Rios had brought to the hospital for her. She didn't want to tell her mom about what had happened. Not yet. Nate wasn't sure that was a wise decision, but it wasn't his to make.

Wolfsinger sat in a plain wooden chair, his fingers laced together and placed against the back of his head. It was a common gesture for the sheriff when he was strategizing. K-9 Bubba had earned some chew time for his good work. He lay on the floor, a plastic chew toy in the shape of a rainbow trout held between his paws. He gnawed at it with his side teeth, his tail wagging happily as the toy squeaked.

"The question is, *why* was that guy so desperate?" Rios said, adding to her earlier comment.

"Somebody probably put pressure on him to clean up the mess he and his idiot partner made," Nate said. "They talked when they should have kept their mouths shut and then made a mess of things when they went after Lily."

"That would be my guess, too." Wolfsinger dropped his hands from the back of his head down to his lap. "But we need to give the detectives time to do their work before we decide we've got it all figured out."

Nate stopped pacing. He very much wanted a shot at interrogating the jerk they'd caught this afternoon, but he was still officially on leave. Sheriff Wolfsinger and a couple of detectives had already tried talking to the homicidal driver, but he hadn't given up any information. Not even his name. He'd been fingerprinted and photographed, so they'd be able to identify him eventually.

"I'd like to be at the stakeout at Torrent Trucking tonight," Rios said to Wolfsinger.

He nodded. "I was planning on it."

"Keep me updated on what happens," Nate said. He was anxious to get the criminal operation closed down and see whoever was directing the attacks on Lily locked up.

"We'll keep you in the loop." Sheriff Wolfsinger turned to Lily. "You're still in serious danger. The two men we've caught so far are just the tip of the iceberg. Having them in custody will make their criminal employers nervous or angry or both. They're going to double their efforts to track you down. You can't let your guard down and you can't go back to your normal life. Not yet."

Nate felt his gut tighten.

He wanted to keep her safe. Wanted to *do* something to fix things for her. Frustration stirred up old, bitter memories. There had been so many times in his life when he'd wanted to make things better for someone, but couldn't. The universe wasn't under his control and sometimes that was very hard to accept.

Lily looked at him and he felt as if he was still crossing uneven ground even though he was standing still. He'd found a measure of balance in his life and she was messing it up. He wanted to do something to lighten her load and make her happy. She deserved that.

And then he'd let her be on her way.

Nate knew his limitations. His childhood had been chaos. Waking up to find his mom passed out on the kitchen floor. A string of "uncles" passing through the house who weren't shy about letting a hopeful little boy know he was a nuisance. Birthdays forgotten and Christmases not celebrated. Nate didn't know the things other men seemed to intuitively know about being a husband and father. He'd missed that boat.

There was a quiet knock on Wolfsinger's office door and Deputy Rios walked over to open it. Bubba continued to chew on his toy, but managed to watch Rios's every move at the same time.

A plainclothes detective stepped into the office and closed the door behind him. He gave one quick nod of greeting directed to everyone in the room before turning to Wolfsinger. "We've got some information back on your gunmen. Also, somebody's here from the district attorney's office to help with deals and charges, depending on whether we want to go with a carrot or stick approach to get information out of them."

Wolfsinger stood. "Rios, you and Bubba get something to eat and get ready for a long night." He turned to Nate. "You're still officially on leave. I can assign a couple of deputies to protect Lily and we can tuck her away in a safe house in town."

"No. I'll take care of her."

"Nate, you did good work in Phoenix. Three different people from Phoenix PD have called to tell me about it. They also told me it was an intense assignment. You've earned some time to unwind."

Lily made a scoffing sound. "Looks as if I've already gotten in the way of that."

Nate turned to her. "You're welcome to stay at the ranch as long as you want. I can keep you safe."

She nodded. "I'd like to stay there."

The sheriff let out a sigh. "All right. I'll make sure there's always a deputy patrolling the roads around the Blue Spruce. If you get even a hint of trouble, Nate, you call it in."

"Yes, sir."

Wolfsinger turned to Lily and glanced at her leg. "Make sure you follow the doctor's orders so you heal up properly. And do what Nate tells you to stay safe."

Lily looked at Nate and rolled her eyes. Then a slight, tired smile played across her lips.

Nate smiled in return. It felt as if the two of them were partners. For now.

"Between the stakeout and the interrogations, maybe we'll get things wrapped up tonight," Wolfsinger said, glancing at everyone around the room. "My concern, though, is that we're looking at something much bigger than just the two yahoos we have in custody and a few people stealing cargo." He took in a deep breath and blew it out. "If we really are looking at a large-scale organized-crime operation, Lily might have accidentally stirred up a hornet's nest."

"It wasn't easy, but I did it." Lily disconnected her phone and set it on the bench seat beside her in Nate's truck, glad *that* conversation was over. "I convinced Mom I'm okay. And I told her Sheriff Wolfsinger assigned extra patrol coverage on Penny's street just in case." Lily had asked for that before she left his office, and the sheriff had agreed.

They were riding along the hard-packed dirt road that led to the ranch.

"And your mom knows you're safe and you'll be staying at the Blue Spruce Ranch for a while longer?" Nate asked.

"Yep."

Wipers slapped rhythmically across the front windshield of the truck, pushing aside the cold, slushy rain that had been falling since they'd left the sheriff's department complex twenty minutes ago.

Nate slowed and turned onto the driveway leading up to the main house at the Blue Spruce. Instead of going directly to the house, though, he pulled into a small barn and parked. "Wait in the truck. I'll drive you up to the house in a minute."

Lily got out of the truck.

"I'm tired of sitting," she said when Nate came around to help her. The pain medication had worn off faster than she'd expected. The searing ache in her leg made her wobbly and she needed to steady herself against the truck's doorframe for a minute.

Nate stood in front of her with his hands out to catch her if she fell. "Want to get back in the truck?"

"Nope." She blew a strand of hair away from her face. "But let's just stand here a minute."

"Sure."

A motion-sensor light in the ceiling had clicked on when they'd pulled into the barn. The place looked like a storage space for stuff that didn't belong anywhere else. Car parts sat on a shelf behind the front end of a small tractor. Snowshoes and mountain bikes hung from pegs on the wall. Fishing poles were tied to rafters in the ceiling.

"Will Deputy Rios or somebody else call and tell you what's happening at the stakeout tonight?" she asked.

"No. They'll have a lot more on their minds than reporting to me." After making sure Lily wasn't going to topple over, Nate walked to a corner and pulled out some wooden crates and a trash can. He dropped in snow chains, bricks, chunks of wood and other random objects.

"What are you doing?" Lily called out when there was a break in all the racket.

"Roadblocks. I'll set them up in the driveway and around the house." Nate walked back toward her. "It's not enough to keep anyone out, but it will slow them down and give us some warning if anyone tries to come after you tonight."

Lily hugged herself. "Why aren't you a detective? The way you and Sheriff Wolfsinger interact seems like something beyond what a typical patrol officer does."

"I was a military policeman in the army for a few

years. When I got out and came back to Copper Mesa, a basic deputy position was the only job available with the sheriff's department. So I applied for it." He glanced at her leg. "Let's get you back in the truck and I'll drive you to the house."

"It's stopped raining," she said with a glance outside. "And it's not that far. I want to try to walk. Sitting actually hurts more."

They stepped outside into the blue twilight. The cool air felt good. Maybe it would help clear her mind.

Nate bent his arm, holding his elbow out toward her. It was an old-fashioned, courtly kind of gesture. She linked her arms through his and he pulled her closer, letting her lean into his strength and helping her walk.

This would *not* help clear her mind. Not at all. The feel of his muscles in his arms and chest made it hard to think. As did the faint cedar scent of his aftershave.

Walking slowly toward the house, they passed by several pine trees. Rainwater dripped off the branches and needles. It smelled like Christmas.

"Your transfer," she said. "Painted Rock. Spill the details."

She'd been watching his face and she immediately regretted asking. He took a deep breath and looked down, the slight smile vanishing from his face.

"Painted Rock is a cute little town, though," she said, giving him an out. Her story was humiliating, but she suddenly knew with cold certainty that his story was much worse.

"You know how my mom was," he said.

She did. The poor woman was wraith-thin and typically dressed in dirty jeans and a shabby T-shirt. She wandered all over town, sometimes in the street. She'd show up at high school football games, pathetically trying to bum a beer off teenagers.

That had to be heartbreaking for Nate. Over and over, she chose her love for alcohol and oblivion over her love for her son. Nate was known for being pretty wild, too. But then he became friends with Joseph and started hanging around the Suh family. And eventually he'd moved up here to the Blue Spruce Ranch.

"I tried my whole life to help my mom, but I couldn't," Nate said quietly. "I was spiraling down the same path she was following until I found faith. Over time I realized I had value as a child of God, even if my mom didn't value me so much. After high school I had to get out of town for a while. Had to get away from *her* for a while." He took a deep breath.

Lily felt a quivering in her own chest. The uncertainty she'd felt growing up was nothing compared to what he'd been through.

"While I was away my mom fell in with yet another group of 'friends.' They were into drugs as much as booze. Imagined themselves big-time dealers. One night there was an exchange of money and drugs at a fast-food restaurant in town. They were probably high or desperate to get high. One guy starts shooting, then another. Bullets fly and my mom catches one through the center of her chest. She was already gone by the time the ambulance arrived."

"You don't have to finish the story," Lily said softly.

"Please listen," Nate said. "There are rumors going around that just aren't true. Accusations that almost cost me my job."

"Okay." She'd eventually heard about his mom, but she'd been away at college when it actually happened.

"I didn't come back to Copper Mesa for revenge, despite what some people have said." He turned to her, and in the moonlight she could see an earnestness in his eyes that was so opposite his usual suspicion it made her heart ache.

"When I came back for my mom's funeral, I realized how much I love it here. I still had a year to go in the army, but I started thinking about the cops back here and how much they'd helped me. I remember one handing me a jacket on the street one day when I was about ten and playing outside. More than one bought me a hamburger over the years. They brought stuff at Christmas. I wanted to do something like that for kids in the same situation."

Lily didn't know what to say. Her arm was wrapped around him as he helped her walk. She gave him a squeeze.

"The Oso County sheriff's department doesn't have a large number of employees or much turnover. I'd had experience and training that would have gotten me a higher rank and a detective's badge anywhere else. But I took the job that was available here. I got out in the community and people started to tell me things about what happened with my mom. And who was involved."

"Wasn't someone arrested after she was killed?"

"Nobody was prosecuted. There wasn't much in the way of evidence and everyone had vanished by the time the cops arrived. As I learned new information, I relayed it to Sheriff Wolfsinger. He put a couple of detectives back on the case and eventually the creeps who were responsible for my mother's death were brought to justice."

"How do you mean 'brought to justice'?" Lily was

trying to figure out how any of this could get Nate into trouble.

Nate looked at her and quirked an eyebrow. "I didn't shoot them, if that's what you're asking."

"Okay." Lily looked away. "I guess that's kinda what I was asking." All this must have happened while she was wrapped up in her own little world with her former fiancé, Kevin.

"The dealers were prosecuted, but the defense claimed I had come back to town seeking revenge. That I had set up the perpetrators. That I had listened to lies and planted evidence."

"And there are people in Copper Mesa who believe that?"

"Yes. But the prosecutors did a good job. So did the detectives and forensics people. They shredded the defense's claims and the perps went to prison for a long time."

"And your transfer?"

"People like to stir things up. The accusations got pretty crazy and interfered with me doing my job. Sheriff Wolfsinger kept me from getting fired, but I had to accept a transfer to Painted Rock."

"That's so unfair," Lily said.

"Ben Wolfsinger stuck his neck out for me," Nate said. "I prefer to focus on how fortunate I am to work for someone like that." He helped her up the porch steps to the house. "Let's get inside. Anybody could be watching us from the surrounding ridges. And as slow as you're moving, you're an easy target."

"It looks like you have things under control here," Nate said a half hour after he got Lily inside the house.

"I believe we do," Ellen agreed.

Lily, looking exhausted, nodded her head. "Snug as a bug." Nate had dragged an easy chair from the living room into the kitchen, where Lily was sitting with her leg propped up. Ellen was nearby making southwest chicken with cornmeal dumplings.

Confident Lily was safe and in good hands, Nate was anxious to go outside and get to work. "I'll be out in the stables. Call me when dinner's ready."

The rain had started up again and Nate walked through the chilly drizzle. He went to the barn to load his makeshift roadblocks into the back of his truck. Then he drove down the long driveway to set them in place. He'd much rather be helping out with the stakeout at Torrent Trucking later tonight, but at least he could do this. And he could watch out for Lily.

Once his roadblocks were in place he headed for the stables, where he could make himself useful and still keep an eye on the house.

It was too late in the day to start on any of the big projects he'd promised Ellen he'd take care of, but there were plenty of small things that needed to be done. The grooming tools for the horses could use a good cleaning and a spit shine. He found a pail and some liquid soap, turned on a hot water tap at the deep utility sink and got to work washing them.

A few minutes later he heard a familiar tread of footsteps behind him and a voice call out, "Really? *Now?* You have to clean that stuff right *now?*" He turned to see Gaston looking at him as though he'd lost his mind.

Nate was used to the look and it didn't rile him. Strangers might be intimidated by Gaston's occasionally glowering demeanor, but anybody who knew him just shrugged it off. Nate got back to work.

"I saw your barricades in the driveway." Gaston strode over to him. "That's not a bad idea. If you want to put out some more, I can help you."

A horse snorted and stirred in a stall a few feet away. The sound was familiar and comforting to Nate, as were the scents of hay and horse and the oiled leather tack.

"I'm almost done," Nate said. "I'll be back up at the house in a few minutes."

"Okay." Gaston reached for some of the cleaning supplies Nate had left in the stable's work area and put them away in the cabinets.

Gaston could come across as contrary, and he sometimes was, but Nate knew he had a good heart and it was simply the way he dealt with worry. Gaston worried about everybody. Nearly all the time. Maybe it was related to the dysfunctional family he'd run away from as a boy, but it was unlikely anyone would ever figure him out. Gaston didn't talk much about his past.

He was a runaway who'd shown up at the ranch one day promising he would work hard enough to earn his keep. Bud and Ellen had officially taken him in as a foster child just before Nate had come to live with them. The two boys were nearly the same age, with Gaston being a year older. They loathed each other at first sight. After a few slugfests they grew tolerant of one other. Eventually they became as close as brothers. When it came to this situation with Lily, Gaston would have Nate's back. He could be sure of that.

"Don't worry," Nate said. "I'm ready for trouble." Never mind that he'd spent years as a military policeman and was now a deputy sheriff, he often had to prove himself to his prickly "older brother." He pushed aside his jacket so Gaston could see the pistol riding on his hip.

"All right." Gaston sighed. "I guess you know what you're doing."

"What do you want me to do, walk around like a sentry with a rifle on my shoulder?" Nate dried his hands on a shop towel and then put the clean horse-grooming tools back where they belonged. "Too bad we don't have an actual working gate across the ranch entrance. Now would be the time to close it."

"Bud and Ellen have always been concerned about making people feel welcome," Gaston said. "Not keeping them out."

And, sweet dispositions aside, Bud and Ellen were perfectly capable of taking care of themselves.

"This might not be the most secure place in the world," Nate said, "but I had to take Lily somewhere. I couldn't just leave her on her own." He emptied the bucket he'd been using into the sink. "She was Joseph Suh's tutor in high school." Once Nate had decided Gaston was tolerable, he'd introduced him to his friends in high school, including Joseph. Like Nate, Gaston had a fledgling faith that was nurtured by Bud and Ellen. Joseph and his family had been welcoming to him.

"I didn't say you shouldn't have brought her here," Gaston said. "I don't remember her from back in the day, though."

"She kept a low profile."

Gaston shook his head. "Too bad this didn't happen earlier in the year before we cut everybody loose for the season." From spring until late summer, they had a dozen cowboys working the ranch. This late into the fall, they were down to just the skeleton crew of Bud, Ellen, Gaston and Nate, when he had the time to come by and help.

A loud thump caught Nate's attention and he turned to see his big orange cat jump from a low wooden cross-beam in the ceiling onto the shelf of an open stall door and then to the ground. Hank liked the horses and they liked him, so he made a point of visiting them often. It was also a good place for him to hunt mice.

"Hey, buddy, how you doing?" Hank meandered over at the sound of Nate's voice and Nate scratched the cat's ears.

"Is there any chance Lily knows something more about who's after her than she's telling you?" Gaston asked.

"At first I thought she might," Nate said, straightening back up. "But now I don't think so."

"Why not?"

Hank wound back and forth between Nate's feet. Nate picked him up, tucked the cat's substantial weight into the crook of his arm and scratched beneath his chin. "Just being around Lily and talking to her about her past and her life made me drop my suspicions," Nate said. "There's no sign she's come into any substantial money. She hasn't tried to get away on her own. She's scared."

"So you think her boss is involved in any of this?"

"I don't know for sure yet." Nate set Hank on the ground and the cat meowed in protest.

"You seem pretty attached to her," Gaston said.

"*Him*, you mean," Nate said, looking down at his cat.

Gaston made a scoffing sound. "You know that's not who I'm talking about."

"You have an overactive imagination."

"I don't think I do," Gaston said.

"I'm not looking for a relationship and neither is she." So maybe there was a little chemistry between them. That didn't prove anything. He'd felt chemistry before and the relationships didn't work out. And if Lily thought she was a little bit interested in him, she'd realize soon enough her attraction was based on what he could do to protect her. That was all it was.

"I'm just not interested," Nate finally said to end the conversation and get Gaston to drop the subject. "She's not my type."

"Huh," Gaston said. "Well, if you say so." He crossed his arms, leaned against a doorjamb and winked. "I think she's cute."

An angry flash of heat shot across the surface of Nate's skin. "She doesn't need anybody hitting on her right now," he snapped. "Even if things get cleared up tonight and go back to normal tomorrow, she's still got a lot on her plate. She works three jobs, you know." Hadn't she said all she wanted to do was work her way out of debt? Hadn't she said she didn't want to make time for a social life right now?

He glanced over to see Gaston grinning at him.

His jaw tightened.

Fortunately, the short, squat, bowlegged form of Bud appeared in a doorway before Nate could say or do anything he might regret. Icy water droplets trailed down the shoulders of Bud's jacket. The rain must have started freezing again.

"Boys, come on back in the house. It's time to eat."

"I'll be there in a few minutes," Nate said, sliding his gaze toward Gaston. It might be best if he stayed and swept or cleaned or did something to burn off the rush of aggravation that made him want to punch his "brother."

Gaston's grin grew even wider.

Nate reached for a broom, grasping the handle so tight his knuckles turned white. A couple of years ago he'd acknowledged the reality that he wasn't cut out for a wife and a family. That acceptance had brought a measure of peace into his life and he wanted to keep it. He needed a few extra minutes to remind himself of that before he saw Lily again.

"Ellie has supper on the table," Bud drawled, looking at Nate as if he couldn't believe what Nate had just said. "You can come tell her you'd rather sweep the stall than eat supper with us if you want to. *I'm* not telling her that."

Ellen had definite ideas about the importance of everyone sitting down to dinner together. She was pretty vocal about it.

Nate looked at the broom in his hand and finally put it away. It wouldn't be fair to create tension over something that was his problem.

"Now, boys, this is the way I see it," Bud began as they left the stables and headed toward the house. "Nate, you get some sleep tonight because you'll have plenty to do tomorrow. Gaston and I can stay up and keep an eye on things until sunup, just in case."

"Which one of us is keeping an eye on Lily?" Gaston asked with a grin.

"Shut up," Nate snapped.

Bud chuckled, avoiding eye contact with both his boys.

Just outside the house Nate glanced again at Gaston and saw the focused determination in his eyes. Then he turned to Bud, who gave him a nod. They might joke around a little bit, but they understood the seriousness of the situation. They'd keep an eye on things.

Nate had made the right decision bringing Lily to the ranch. She was safe. For now.

EIGHT

Nate turned his truck onto the driveway of the Blue Spruce Ranch without hitting the brake, sliding sideways before recovering control and racing up to the front of the house. He finally had news but he didn't want to share it over the phone.

Last night had passed uneventfully. Nate had been up before sunrise and driven into Copper Mesa early, but the deputies that had worked the Torrent Trucking stakeout were either off their shift and home sleeping, or still on shift but not authorized to give him any details. Sheriff Wolfsinger had ordered a tight lid on information until he'd had time to sort things out.

Nate had waited impatiently until midday, when the sheriff was finally willing to talk to him. Now he was anxious to share what he'd learned with Lily. It wasn't great news, exactly, but it showed that investigators had a new lead on where to focus their attention. Maybe it would help her feel less cast adrift.

She'd been quiet at dinner last night. When he'd risked a few glances in her direction, she'd been staring down at her plate rather than eating every single time. Considering everything she'd been through that day, it wasn't a surprise. Still, she'd offered to help clean up the kitchen after dinner. Ellen turned down her offer, drafting Bud and Gaston to do the job instead. Lily had then turned in for the night, even though it was early.

Now Bud stepped down from the front porch and walked over as Nate hustled out of the truck. "I saw that fast driving. And, boy, if you knock down a section of fence you'll have to put it back up."

"Yes, sir." Nate had knocked down quite a few sections of fence along the road and the driveway back in his time.

"You must have learned something interesting," Bud said as they both started walking toward the house.

"I did."

"Well, let's get in the house and find Ellen. She'll give it to me good if you tell me something important and she has to hear it secondhand."

"Actually, I was hoping to tell Lily first."

Bud cleared his throat as they reached the front door. "Well, of course I meant to include Lily in the conversation, too."

It felt good to get out of the cold and inside the house. A butter-and-cinnamon scent greeted him and he could hear Lily and Ellen talking in the kitchen. Ellen was an expert at keeping somebody busy and getting their mind off their worries. Good thing she and Lily enjoyed each other's company. It looked like Lily was going to have to hide out at the Blue Spruce for a while longer.

"Look who the cat dragged in," Bud called out from behind Nate. While Ellen's expertise lay in keeping people busy and feeling useful, Bud was skilled at humor and lifting spirits with optimism and a warm smile. There were people in town who misread his demeanor, particularly when coupled with his round figure and moon-shaped face, and they thought he was either simple or shallow. Their opinions couldn't be further from the truth. Ellen had chosen wisely when she agreed to marry Nate's uncle. But then Bud had chosen wisely, as well.

While Ellen greeted Nate, Bud sidled up to the granite-topped kitchen island and delicately selected one oatmeal cookie off of a plate. With his other hand he quickly grabbed four more. Ellen rolled her eyes and shook her head, making Nate laugh.

"I've got news," Nate said to Lily, a little surprised at how happy she looked. Maybe ranch life agreed with her. Or maybe she'd just taken one of the painkillers the doctor had given her. She seemed to be moving around the kitchen pretty well despite her injured leg.

"I've got news, too," Lily said, beaming.

"Okay." Nate realized he still had his cowboy hat on and he took it off. "Ladies first."

"I'm going back to work!"

"What?" What could she possibly mean? Had Ellen hired her to do something around the ranch? Maybe help with housekeeping or taking care of the animals? She and Bud could always find a paying job for someone if they really needed it. Even if the pay was simply room and board. Lily had made it clear she was determined to earn her own way. "What are you talking about?"

"I'm going back to Torrent Trucking. I can return to work tomorrow."

Nate felt his blood turn cold. "That's not possible."

"But it is! Business is back to normal and I'm supposed to report first thing in the morning."

Nate shook his head. "That's not right." In fact,

something was very wrong. That didn't mesh at all with what he'd finally learned from Sheriff Wolfsinger.

"It is!" she insisted with a broad smile on her face. "Bryan Torrent came through on his promise to have new security measures installed. He paid a fortune to have it put in quickly. He's also hired a private security firm so there'll be on-site guards."

"No." Nate shook his head, feeling as if the solid ground was sinking beneath his feet.

"It's okay," Lily said quickly.

She looked so earnest and hopeful in those black-framed glasses it made Nate's heart ache. And it made him want to strangle whoever had lied to her.

"You might need to drive me back and forth for a few days," she continued, picking up steam in her enthusiasm. "Or maybe one of the security guys can do it."

"Please tell me you read about this online," Nate said tightly. He knew from experience that news hastily posted online was oftentimes incomplete or inaccurate.

"No, I didn't read it online. Eddie Drake called me. You remember him, you met him. The red-haired guy. He helps manage the place and maintains a lot of the tech stuff."

And he'd badgered Lily to go on a date with him. Yeah, Nate remembered the guy.

"You talked to him?"

"Yes." Her smile faded and she looked around uncertainly. Bud and Ellen looked worried. They didn't know what exactly was wrong, but they were experts at reading the expression on Nate's face. They knew he wasn't happy.

Nate snapped his attention to Bud. "Where's Gaston?"

"He's in the office working on something." Bud stepped out of the kitchen and hollered down the hallway. Nate heard Gaston reply a few seconds later. Bud came back into the kitchen. "He's on his way."

"What did you tell Eddie Drake about what you're doing right now?" Nate stepped toward Lily. "Did you tell him where you're staying?"

She lifted her chin, her dark eyes already full of regret. "Why?"

"What did you tell him?" Nate asked more forcefully.

"I don't remember, exactly." She crossed her arms over her chest and backed up to the countertop. She glanced at Ellen before turning back to Nate. "I thought everything was over. Or nearly over. And it's just Eddie." She took a deep breath. "What's wrong?"

"Did you tell him you're staying here?"

"No-o-o." She drew out the word, sounding uncertain. "I told him I was staying with friends and that it was nice to be out of town and up where the air was fresh and the pine trees smelled so good." She blanched.

Yeah, she might not have told Eddie specifically where she was, but she'd given him enough hints. He'd seen Lily and Nate together. Everybody in town knew about Nate's connection to the Blue Spruce. It didn't take a degree in rocket science to put it all together.

"Has Eddie done something wrong?" Lily asked in a thin voice.

"Sheriff Wolfsinger talked to Bryan Torrent while I was at the sheriff's department. It's going to take longer than he thought to get his new security in place. He's keeping the business shut down until he can get that taken care of and he specifically said he wouldn't need you back to work for at least a couple more weeks. Eddie lied to you."

Gaston walked into the kitchen lugging Nate's orange cat. "What do you want?"

"I want you to do a couple of things after we leave and then I want you to stay right here in the house."

"Okay."

Nate and Gaston had a history of backing each other even before they knew all the details. Sometimes explanations just had to wait.

"We're leaving?" Lily asked.

"The district attorney's office came up with some serious charges with lengthy prison terms for Jack Covert, the guy who was wearing the hoodie, and Blaine Revel, the man who held the gun on you at the Starlight Mart and then tried to kill you at the plant and pottery store. The prosecutors working with Sheriff Wolfsinger came up with a plea deal for both of those idiots if they'd give up any useful information. Both admitted to being involved in cargo theft. Both mentioned Eddie Drake as their contact person in the crime ring."

Lily put her hand to her mouth.

Nate sighed. "The stakeout was a bust. They watched Torrent Trucking all night but nobody showed up. So early in the morning, the deputies went to Eddie's house to talk to him. He was gone."

Lily's face turned red and tears formed in the corners of her eyes. Nate hated having to tell her things that upset her, but he steeled himself and continued. There was just one small bit of information left. "Sheriff Wolfsinger brought Bryan Torrent in for a chat. Torrent said Eddie had originally applied for his job online, had excellent references and lots of experience. He claimed to have no prior connection to Eddie."

Lily shook her head. "I'm so stupid."

"No, you're not," Nate said.

"I should have—"

"Everybody makes mistakes," Nate interrupted. "Let's focus on a solution. Gaston, call Lonnie and see if he and his brothers can hang out here for a few days."

"On it." He got out his phone.

"I'm not completely useless," Bud grumbled. "I can take care of things around here."

"I know. But we're going to need extra people up here so we can have someone on the lookout twenty-four hours a day." Nate reached out and squeezed Bud's shoulder. "Eddie, or whoever he's working with, might come here looking for Lily. I'd hate to see what would happen if they ran into you or Ellen. I don't want you three dealing with this alone after we leave."

Bud nodded and Nate let go of his shoulder. Nate turned to Gaston, who was already off the phone. "As soon as we get out of here, I want you to block the drive at the road with something. The full barrels and crates I put out there won't be enough if someone's determined to get to the house. Park a horse trailer out there. A front loader. Something big. And remember there's a deputy assigned to the area around the ranch. If anything happens here call 911 and you'll have help right away."

"You keep talking about us leaving," Lily said. "Where are we going?"

Nate turned back to her. "I have some friends in Painted Rock. If we can get to them, we might be safe."

"But won't we be putting them in danger?"

"We might be. But they'll be ready for it."

She dropped her gaze. "You can't be certain of that."

"Yeah, I can. These friends are a little unusual. Have you ever heard of a Christian motorcycle outreach group called Vanquish the Darkness?"

She lifted her gaze. "Don't they help veterans and support a couple of children's charities?"

"Yes." Nate nodded. "That and a whole lot more."

"We're almost at the crossroads by the Starlight Mart," Nate said into his phone.

They were in a truck he'd borrowed from Gaston in hopes it would make them less likely to be recognized if Eddie or any of his criminal friends were looking for them. Nate glanced at Lily with his eyebrows slightly raised, as if he thought she might freak out or something. Lily forced a small, grim smile in acknowledgment that they were indeed back to the spot where she was nearly murdered just a couple of nights ago. Her stomach sank and she felt the blood drain from her face, but she thought she did a pretty good job of appearing calm.

Nate turned his gaze back to the road. Lily could see his jaw muscles tense.

"I'm getting ready to turn onto the highway up to Painted Rock," he said into his phone, continuing his conversation. "We should be there in less than an hour."

Nate had insisted they leave the Blue Spruce Ranch immediately, giving Lily only fifteen minutes to repack her travel bag and be ready to go. Once they were under way, he'd called Sheriff Wolfsinger and told him about Lily's conversation with Eddie. Then he'd told Lily he wanted to call someone from Vanquish the Darkness and give them a heads-up they were coming.

There was no denying Lily was running for her life. Just a few days ago she was worried about a lot of things. Her broken engagement. Flunking out of college. Being a financial burden to her mom. They were real problems, but they were fixable. Much of the damage had been done to her pride. Hard to believe she'd ever thought that was such a huge deal.

She shook her head and glanced out the window. For the longest time, she'd convinced herself she could control her future if she made good plans and had the discipline to stick to them. Then she'd thought she'd ruined her future by giving in to the temptation to shake off all those rules and live in the moment.

Somewhere along the line she'd lost that part of her faith that reminded her God was in control and had a plan for her. She could plan and work and have goals. She *should* do that. But ultimately the twists and turns her life would take weren't all determined by her. She blew out a breath, a little unnerved by that reminder, but also, in an unexpected way, strengthened.

Nate ended his call.

"That was Elijah Morales I was talking to," he said as he made the turn north. The two-lane stretch of asphalt would take them across an expanse of scrubby high desert that looked flat but actually rose steadily in elevation. After crossing it, they'd reach the bottom of a winding road that would take them up into the thickly forested mountains and eventually to the small town of Painted Rock.

"Elijah brought Vanquish back to life about three years ago after he returned from serving in the Middle East," Nate continued. "He was an army ranger."

Lily was no expert in military affairs, but she knew what a ranger was. "That alone earns him respect."

"It does." Nate checked his mirrors. He'd constantly checked them and kept an eye on surrounding traffic from the moment they'd left the Blue Spruce Ranch. It was midafternoon and traffic outside of Copper Mesa had been sparse. Just a few cars and scattered big-rig trucks.

"I'm a little concerned that this guy doesn't just pass me out here," Nate muttered.

Lily glanced in her side mirror. Even though Nate drove faster than the speed limit—a habit she'd already noticed—a car stayed impatiently close to their tail. Some kind of customized SUV with fat tires and darkened windows.

After a couple of tense minutes it finally did pass them. Once it was several car lengths ahead of them and accelerating, Lily could see Nate's arms and shoulders relax. Then he set a handgun on the bench seat between them. He must have had it tucked somewhere under his coat.

"We're in Gaston's truck and we didn't see anyone behind us driving down the road from the ranch. Do you really think someone could already be following us?" she asked, hoping for some reassurance to help throw off the sense of dread that had settled over her when they'd passed by the Starlight Mart as they made the turn to head north at the crossroads.

"Criminals aren't always dumb or lazy. Or without law-enforcement connections," Nate added grimly.

"So why exactly is Painted Rock safer than anywhere else?" Lily asked. "There are lots of places we could go. Maybe even a different state. And what do you know about Vanquish the Darkness? That's a pretty dramatic name."

Up ahead the SUV that had just passed them hit its brakes and then turned off the highway. Typical. People were always in such a hurry even when they only had a mile or two to go before they turned.

Or maybe he was going to come back up behind them. Lily kept her eyes on her side mirror, hoping the SUV wouldn't reappear. There were plenty of nearly invisible paths leading off the highway out here. Some were private roads leading to houses or trailers not visible from the main road. Others meandered out to illegal dump sites, spots where people liked to camp, or in some cases improvised race tracks.

"A person could have a staging area for stolen cargo anywhere out here," she muttered. "You'd never find them."

"Don't be so sure. There are plenty of men and women out fighting the good fight who are smart and relentless. I got out and rode around on some of these trails back when I was younger and didn't have anything better to do. I could track somebody out here if I had to."

Lily shook her head. "It's overwhelming."

"Not if you have help," Nate insisted. "Let me tell you about Vanquish the Darkness. Joe and Julie Morales started it about thirty years ago. They and some of their friends from church liked to ride and wanted to do something good for people. They formed an outreach group that visited shut-ins and people in the hospital, raised funds for children's programs and made sure veterans knew they weren't forgotten."

"Sounds like a great idea." Lily still had her eyes on

the mirror. She could see for a long distance behind her and the road was still empty.

"They went like gangbusters for a few years but at some point their activities slowed down and finally stopped. I don't know why, but my guess is the members started their families and riding motorcycles most weekends didn't work well with raising little kids."

"I can see that." None of this explained how they could help her and Nate stay safe.

They had crossed the flats and were heading up into the mountains.

"Joe and Julie's son, Elijah Morales, was an army ranger and came home after serving a couple of tours in the Middle East," Nate continued. "He wanted to keep serving in some capacity. At first, he just got together with friends from church to visit veterans in hospitals and other facilities and make sure they were okay. But then they stumbled across people who needed serious help, people who were in danger."

"Okay, but why not call the cops?"

"Oh, they do. But not everybody gets a personal protection plan."

She glanced over at Nate. He looked pointedly at her and she felt her face flush. She turned back to the mirror. Apparently he didn't think of himself as a family man. If Lily got involved with a man again, he would have to want a family like she did. And he'd have to be a lot more reliable than Kevin.

"The resources aren't there to protect citizens around the clock and some people don't have family or friends to take them in until the situation is safe again," Nate added.

Thank You, Lord, Lily prayed. She did have family

and friends to help her out. She stole another look at Nate. Right now she had her own personal protector. A very attractive one, to boot. Not everybody got that.

"Specifically, we're heading for the Morales Ranch," Nate continued. "Not only does the Morales family live and work there, it's also the central hub for Vanquish. They have a network of riders and support people who will show up at a moment's notice. And the main ranch house has a pretty extensive security system, which is why I'm taking you there."

"Do you ever ride with them?"

"When I have time."

It was easy to imagine Nate on a motorcycle. He'd certainly had the look when he first showed up at the Starlight Mart.

"I met them after I got transferred out here about a year ago. I got a call on a traffic incident. A woman had been driven off the road. She was on her way to visit her great-aunt in Painted Rock, who happens to be a neighbor of the Moraleses. She was coming from Las Vegas, where she'd angered a mob attorney. Elijah and some of his Vanquish riders came to her rescue."

The road wound along the side of a mountain. There were stretches where Lily could only see pine trees or exposed rock, but then there were open stretches where she could get a clear view. The ground to the side of the road fell away to a steep drop. Beyond the edge, the flatland where they'd just driven spread out below them. Vibrant red and orange mesas jutted into the skyline in the distance.

"Did the woman from Las Vegas survive?" Lily asked, feeling her throat thicken just a little. Maybe this story had a bad ending.

"She's fine. Her name is Olivia. She and Elijah got married."

A loud bang, like an explosion, rocked the truck.

Lily screamed, her fingers digging into the seat beside her.

Nate fought for control as they swerved across the narrow road.

NINE

The truck slid until its right front tire hit a jut of rock and sent them ricocheting back across the highway, where they finally came to a stop. At least they were on the side of the road that pressed up against the mountain. Heart pounding in his chest, Nate looked over at Lily. The sight of a spray of blood across her cheek stole his breath for several seconds. Then he saw that her side window had been completely blown out.

"Ha," Lily said. Not a laugh, but a stunned exhalation. It sounded as if she was reaching for a word but couldn't grab hold of it.

"Where were you hit?" Nate quickly unbuckled his seat belt and moved toward her.

Her face was drained of color, her dark brown eyes looking bigger than usual behind the glasses that sat slightly askew on the bridge of her nose.

When she didn't answer he started checking her for injuries, carefully brushing aside the bits of safety glass from her side window. Fortunately, it had done its job and not splintered into deadly shards. The blood on her cheek came from a small cut just in front of her ear.

"I'm not hit," she finally said, her voice oddly calm.

She had to be in shock. He glanced at the windshield and saw a hole surrounded by a spiderweb of cracks just above the dashboard where the bullet had passed through.

Ambush was Nate's first thought. But from where? There were foothills with off-roader riding trails etched all through them down below this stretch of the highway. Maybe someone had shot at them from one of the foothills. Or maybe from the side of the road. He twisted in the seat to look in every direction around them, but he couldn't see anybody. He turned back to Lily. "I'm going to unfasten your seat belt."

"Okay." Her voice sounded robotic. He didn't blame her for being scared. He was scared, too. Maybe they were surrounded. Maybe somebody was getting ready to close in on them.

He unbuckled her seat belt and gently tugged down on her arm. "Slide to the floorboard and tuck down as low as you can. Stay out of sight."

"Okay." This time she started to move. She was getting her wits back. Good for her.

Nate already had his phone in his hand. His door was facing the mountainside, nearly pressed against the wall of rock. He opened the door, slid out and crouched down, holding his pistol in one hand while he dialed 911 with the other.

Nothing happened with his phone. He glanced at the screen. No bars. No reception. No surprise. He knew there were stretches along this switchback up the mountain where it was impossible to get reception without a satellite phone. And he hadn't gotten one yet because the radio in his patrol car worked just fine out here.

Watching him, Lily reached into her purse on the seat

for her phone and tried it, too. She looked up at him and shook her head. No reception, either.

The coughing sound of a struggling car engine followed by the squeal of brakes caught Nate's attention. A weathered blue van had rounded the bend behind them and slammed to a stop a few yards shy of Gaston's battered truck.

"Put your head down," Nate commanded, keeping his voice calm while his heart raced in his chest. He pulled out a backup pistol he'd placed under the front seat before they'd left the ranch. He set it on the seat and looked at Lily. "If anything happens," he said, "use it."

"Hey, man, are you okay?" The driver of the van got out and started toward him. He was a tall, skinny guy, not much more than a teenager, dressed in a plaid flannel shirt and ripped jeans. He flashed a friendly smile. The passenger in the front seat, a chubbier fellow, got out and followed him holding a soda cup from the Starlight Mart and sipping from a bright orange straw.

They looked harmless. Which meant nothing. They could be shooters who knew exactly how to blend in with their surroundings, how to appear innocent.

"Stop right there," Nate called out, still trying to assess the situation and figure out what had happened to him and Lily in the truck. Somebody must have taken the shot with a sniper rifle from a good distance away. Maybe it was one of these guys and they were here to confirm the kill. Or maybe it was the missing Eddie Drake and he was nearby, waiting for his chance to shoot again.

The good Samaritans dropped their smiles at Nate's less-than-friendly greeting. They exchanged confused glances. When they turned back to Nate, they both looked afraid. Which didn't mean that they actually were. That could be an act.

Nate watched their hands. He didn't see any guns, but that could just mean they kept them tucked away out of sight.

He lifted his hand so they could see the pistol he held. Just in case they had any ideas.

"What's going on?" Lily asked in a soft voice.

"Two men are walking up the road," Nate quietly answered.

"If you really want to help," Nate called out to the men who'd stopped and now stood staring at him as if they were afraid to move, "go back down the mountain until you get cell reception and call 911."

"Okay, that's cool." The skinny guy vigorously nodded his head and held up his hands in a placating gesture. Then he glanced at his friend, who'd pulled the soda straw out of his mouth, and they both backed toward their van, keeping an eye on Nate the whole time. Once inside it, they made a panicked attempt at a U-turn and had to back up and move forward a couple of times, then they burned rubber and raced back down the mountain.

Their response was not necessarily good news. If neither one of them was the shooter, it meant the shooter was still out there. Maybe even nearby. Possibly with a fix on Lily or Nate right this very minute.

"Are they gone?" Lily asked.

"Yes." Nate turned back toward Gaston's truck. It wasn't going anywhere under its own power. One of the fenders was bashed in far enough that it got in the way of the tire. So the question plaguing Nate now was whether Lily was safer tucked down in the truck, where the shooter couldn't see her, or if having her stay in the truck made her an easier-to-find target.

"Staying scrunched down here is making my thigh hurt," Lily grumbled. "Can I get up now?"

"Sorry." He'd forgotten about her injury. But getting shot would be worse. "Try to stay down there for a few more minutes."

Meanwhile, he scanned the trees around them, feeling uneasy. Not the best cover, but if they could make it just a little farther up the road they'd have cell service again. He'd have to carry Lily. It might be slow going, but it was starting to look like their best option.

Nate's decision was made for him when he heard another car rumbling up the mountainside. He watched until he saw the customized SUV that had passed them earlier. It stopped a few car lengths down the road, idled for a few seconds and then slowly backed out of sight. The driver cut the engine.

Weird.

Nate stepped around the truck, closer to the driver's side door he'd left open, so he could take cover behind it if he had to. Then he waited to see if this was another, more cautious Good Samaritan. Nate couldn't see what was happening and that worried him. A lot.

Lily shifted her weight and started climbing up from the floorboard onto the truck's bench seat.

"Wait," Nate said quietly.

"For what?" Lily snapped. "My leg hurts."

"I think someone else is coming up the road."

Either she didn't hear him or she didn't realize the danger she was in. She kept her head down but she still continued to climb up onto the seat. Nate moved into the juncture where the door was attached to the truck, positioning his body so that anyone or anything would have to go through him to get to her.

A bullet pinged off the exposed rock on the mountainside just behind his shoulder, sending rock fragments flying. Nate hadn't even heard the report of the shot being fired. The shooter was using a silencer.

"Get down!" He lunged into the truck, throwing himself on top of Lily and wrapping his arms around her head.

"What's happening?" she cried out in a tearful voice.

Nate rose up and looked out the back window. Someone was walking toward them, but he stayed in the shadows by the side of the road. It looked like the figure of a man. Eddie Drake? He couldn't tell. The man was dressed in camo, a bandanna tied across the lower half of his face and a black beanie pulled down low across his forehead. He was carrying a rifle.

Nate slid out of the truck, staying low and using the truck to keep his body hidden from the gunman. He flicked the safety off the pistol in his hand, mentally kicking himself for not having brought a rifle. He would have to let the man get closer before he'd be in range of Nate's handgun. The last thing he wanted was for Lily to get caught in the middle of a gunfight, but he had no choice.

Lily shifted so she could see Nate.

He nodded toward the other gun on the seat. "Do you know how to use that?"

"No."

He reached for the gun and made sure the safety was off. "If something happens to me, use it. Do the best you can."

"I will."

This time he could hear the steel in her voice, the courage that had saved her life more than once before. It made him feel better.

Nate watched and waited to see what the man with the rifle would do. There was no telling what other weapons he might have or who else might be with him. But the second he pointed that rifle toward Nate, Nate would take a shot at him. He couldn't risk getting hurt and leaving Lily unprotected.

Wind stirred through the tops of the pine trees, making a sound similar to waves reaching the shore. Nate kept watching and listening. Someone else could also be closing in on them from a different direction. He concentrated so hard he could hear his own heartbeat thumping in his ears.

And then he heard something different. An engine. More than one. Motorcycles.

The man with the rifle must have heard the sounds at the same time Nate did. He backed away in the direction he'd come from, and a few seconds later Nate heard the SUV's engine start up and fade away. Shortly after, a string of shiny black-and-chrome motorcycles came into view on the road up ahead.

Nate breathed a sigh of relief and stood up.

The man riding the lead motorcycle and a second rider just behind him pulled up close to Nate. The others pulled off to the side and waited, engines idling.

"You all right?" The leader glanced at the truck. "What happened?"

"That's Lily in the front seat," Nate said in response to Elijah Morales. "Take care of her." He turned to the other, younger, man beside Elijah. "Jonathan, give me your bike."

"Why do you want my brother's bike?" Elijah asked, calmly crossing his arms over his chest.

"Someone shot out the window on the truck and we crashed." Now that Nate knew Lily would be safe, his fear was replaced with burning fury. He'd had enough of hiding. "Then the guy came up the hill and took a shot at me. I'm going after him."

"Whoa." Elijah held up a gloved hand. "You don't need to chase after anybody right now." Nate glared at him, but Elijah didn't back down.

"Why not?" Nate spat out the words.

"Because that would be a stupid, hotheaded move." He tilted his head slightly. "And that's not your style."

"It's a good thing you came along when you did," Lily said to the biker standing in front of her.

"This is Elijah Morales." Nate made the introductions between Elijah and Lily.

Lily looked into the nearly black eyes of the dark-skinned man with small scars across his face. He wore his hair in a buzz cut and he stood and moved with a military bearing. "I'm glad to meet you," she said. "Especially after what just happened."

That spacey, detached feeling of shock was gone and her leg was starting to throb.

"I'm happy to meet you, too." His smile was slight but the warmth in his voice sounded sincere. He gestured toward his fellow riders, who had parked along the side of the road. "And these are a few other members of Vanquish the Darkness."

One of the riders stayed close to Elijah, the one named Jonathan. The others stayed farther back, intently watching the scene. Lily counted eight of them.

One was a woman. Each of them nodded or waved a greeting. She waved back.

Lily turned back to Elijah and Jonathan, who had both gotten off their bikes. All the other members of Vanquish were still on their motorcycles. "How did you know we needed help?"

Jonathan answered. He was tall and slender with spiky gelled hair and a small tuft of hair below his bottom lip. He looked like he was in his early twenties. "My brother here thought he was going to ride out alone to meet you and escort you to Painted Rock." He hooked a thumb toward Elijah. "He was getting ready to leave right after he spoke to Nate on the phone, but I suggested he wait until we could get a few people together. Just in case there was trouble."

It was starting to sound like Nate and Elijah might be cut from the same cloth.

Elijah glanced at his younger brother and sighed.

"Thank you," Lily said. "You just saved our lives."

Jonathan nodded and Lily could see a slight blush under his dusky skin. "My family is looking forward to having you stay at our ranch for a while."

"You know, we could all be riding right now instead of yammering," Nate snapped at Elijah. He glanced enviously at the Vanquish leader's powerful-looking motorcycle. "Even after we've stood here wasting time for so long I could still catch up with that jerk."

"Not a good idea," Elijah repeated calmly.

Nate glowered in the silence that followed. Lily could see his jaw muscles tense. And then she heard a sound. A siren.

She looked up the road and saw flashing blue and red lights between the trees on the switchback ahead.

A few seconds later a sheriff's department patrol car rounded a corner and came into clear view. A second patrol car followed.

The vehicles stopped just behind the parked Vanquish motorcycles. Deputy Rios got out of the first car. Lily heard Bubba barking excitedly and saw him moving impatiently in the backseat. A second deputy Lily didn't recognize got out of the other patrol car and stepped up beside Rios.

"Get back in your car and let's go," Nate said to Rios when she got closer to him.

"Go where?"

"The idiot who shot at me took off just a few minutes ago. I've seen his vehicle. I can find him."

Rios held up a hand. "Wait. What are you talking about? We just got a call reporting an accident. The guy said he and his buddy stopped to help after they saw a wrecked truck on the road and some big crazy man with a gun threatened them. I'm guessing that's you. Now you're saying someone *shot* at you?"

"First someone shot out Lily's window. I didn't see that shooter. But then a guy drove up here, stopped his SUV, walked up carrying a rifle and took a shot at me. Maybe it's the same shooter. Maybe not." He glanced toward Elijah and his brother. "I know if these guys hadn't showed up I'd be in the middle of a gunfight right now. So let's go get the jerk in the SUV."

Nate tried to step around Rios and get to her patrol car. She was half his size but she got in his way again. "What did the SUV look like? Did you see the plates?"

"He left it in the shadows. I couldn't see the plates." Nate rattled off a description of the SUV. The second deputy started talking into his collar mic and then jogged back to his patrol car.

Nate turned to follow him.

"Nate!" Rios called out. "Stop!"

Lily could see how much respect Nate had for his fellow deputy when he actually stopped and turned around to listen to what she had to say.

"You don't have to do this by yourself," she snapped. "Glenn is talking to Dispatch." At that point the deputy pulled away in his patrol car and shot down the highway.

"Everybody will be looking for the SUV, Nate. Your *friends* in the department will make sure they find it. Though it will probably be a burned-out shell by then. Meanwhile, you've got to take care of yourself. I've never known you to toss aside your common sense and act without thinking." She glanced at Lily, her gaze lingering for a few seconds, and then turned back to him. "Don't start now."

Nate blew out a breath. At some point he'd balled his hands into fists. He unclenched them, nodded at Rios and then walked back to Lily.

"I'm so sorry," he said quietly, leaning down toward her, his breath tickling her ear.

She could feel her heart thudding in her chest. "Sorry? For what? For keeping me alive?"

"What are all of you doing up here, anyway?" Rios asked, walking closer to Nate and Lily and the Morales brothers.

"We're out here helping our brother and sister," Jonathan said exuberantly.

Elijah looked at the ground and shook his head. But Lily could see a slight smile on his lips.

Nate explained why they had to leave the Blue Spruce

Ranch in a hurry and why they were on their way to Painted Rock. "Apparently someone's been watching us since we left," he said. "And it's obvious by now they know where we're going. I'm going to have to come up with another plan."

"Maybe not." Rios chewed her bottom lip for a few seconds. "Normally you live and work up here. Though lately you've been fooling around down in Phoenix while I've done your job for you."

"You just play with your dog and pretend to work," Nate joked back.

Rios smiled. "I'll drive you two to your apartment in Painted Rock. You can sneak out the back of the property and Elijah can drive you to the Morales ranch. The bad guys might not have realized that's your ultimate destination. Especially if they aren't from around here.

"We'll leave some lights on at your place. I'll go to the hardware store and buy a timer so they're off during the day and on for a few hours after dusk. If anyone's watching the apartment they might think you're actually there. It could buy us some time to track down your shooter from the highway and hopefully figure out where Eddie Drake is. Or if he was the actual shooter."

"All right," Nate said. "We'll do things your way for now. But if we don't get results, I'm going to start doing them my way."

TEN

Nate's apartment building was a hacienda-style structure located one street over from what passed for the city center of Painted Rock. The town had started out as a stagecoach relay station and expanded from there, but it still kept its frontier feel after all these years. Nate liked the town well enough, but it didn't feel like home.

He scanned the living room of his apartment, trying to imagine how it looked to Lily. Plain furniture, bare walls, none of the small extras that make a room feel cozy. She probably thought he spent the least amount of time possible here and she'd be right.

He shook his head. Why did he even care what she thought about his place? He was trying to keep her alive. He wasn't dating her. And flying off the handle like he had on the highway after the attack, determined to hunt down the man who'd dared try to hurt Lily, wasn't like Nate at all. He prided himself on keeping a level head. Clearly he needed to take a step back from her, emotionally, and remind himself she was simply an old acquaintance he was helping for the sake of an old friend.

And yet he still couldn't resist watching for her reaction to what she saw in his home. What she might see in *him*.

He stole a glance at her as she scanned the books on his bookcase. Fiction, mostly. Lots of Westerns. If work or life was getting to Nate, he could lose himself better in reading than he ever could in a movie or TV. And it helped still his mind on those nights when he couldn't fall asleep.

Rios was on Nate's landline, updating Sheriff Wolfsinger and getting departmental approval to buy the timers for the lights. The sheriff was well aware of the search for the man, or possibly men, who'd shot at Lily and Nate today, but so far there was no new information.

"I'm heading to the store," Rios said after she got off the phone. She gestured to Bubba and he stood up from his position near a water bowl. "I'll bring back the timers and hook them up."

"Elijah should be by here to pick us up in a few minutes," Nate said, glancing at the screen on his phone. He'd received a text a short time ago. He looked up at Rios. "We'll be gone before you're back. Thanks for your help."

"No problem." Rios turned to Lily. "We'll get these guys. Don't let yourself get discouraged."

"I won't."

"You hungry?" Nate asked Lily after Rios left.

"Kinda."

He walked into the kitchen. "This is my first time back here since I left for Phoenix," he called out to her in the living room. "I don't think I have much here except for snack food."

"That's fine." She walked toward the serving bar between the living room and kitchen. He saw her limping before she pulled back one of the wooden bar stools and sat down with a grimace.

"Your leg hurts," he said. He pulled a couple of glasses down from a cabinet and glanced in the fridge, but decided the orange juice in there was questionable, so he filled the glasses with tap water instead. "I'll grab your purse for you and you can take a pain pill."

"No." She reached over and touched his arm, holding him in place. He froze, not wanting to break contact. Despite every crazy thing that had happened since he ran into her in the Starlight Mart, there was something about Lily that was soothing. Something about her touch that made him feel like he mattered to her and that he mattered as something more than simply a lawman who could help keep her from getting killed.

Which was ridiculous. Obviously he needed to get a grip. He moved his arm away from her hand and opened some cabinet doors. "Why don't you want to take your medicine?"

She didn't move for a few seconds, her expression turning to something that looked like disappointment. Then she sighed and glanced away. "If you've got some over-the-counter pain medicine that would be great. The prescription stuff makes me a little woozy so I don't want to take it until we're at the Morales ranch. Just in case there's more trouble."

He found a pain reliever for her. He also found some canned soup, which didn't sound too thrilling, and some dried noodles. But in the drawer where he normally kept cookies he did find something exciting.

"Chocolate bars, graham crackers and marshmallows?" she said when he set them on the counter in front of her.

"How about s'mores?"

She nodded. "Perfect."

He lined up some graham crackers on a plate and topped them with pieces of chocolate bar, then stabbed a couple of forks into big marshmallows. He turned on the gas stove top and set the marshmallows on fire, waving them a little to keep the smoke from getting to the smoke detector. When they were just right he let Lily blow them out and then smushed them onto the chocolate.

Lily's huge, chocolate-smeared grin after she bit into her s'more gave him an absurd, heart-lifting feeling of accomplishment.

They were both pretty hungry so he made a second round.

"Those were great," she said, wiping the last crumbs from her lips. "Where'd you learn to make them?"

He hesitated. Maybe they'd be friends when all this was over. He would like that. But he needed to know he could talk honestly to her, otherwise what was the point of a friendship? "I learned it from one of my mom's boyfriends. He was around for an entire summer, which was the longest any of them stayed. He liked to sit outside while he drank and talked and looked at the stars at night. And he liked to make s'mores. He was a nice guy."

Nate watched her closely, waiting for a reaction. His past was his past and he had his own perspective on it. Disgust, pity or anything like that would tell him things would never go anywhere between him and Lily. It would prove their worlds were too far apart and it might even be a relief to know that.

She gave him a lingering look. And then she smiled. "Sounds like a good memory."

For him, it actually was. Nate found himself staring at her face and feeling that soothing connection again without even touching her. It felt as if his heart was expanding in his chest.

And then his phone chimed and he looked down at the screen. For a few brief moments he and Lily had been able to forget she was in danger. That respite was over. "Elijah and his wife are waiting out back. Time to go."

Outside, the golden late-afternoon sunshine had turned to purple dusk. Nate and Lily hurried to meet Elijah in his pickup truck in the alley behind the apartments and they quickly lay down in the backseat. Lily's leg hurt, but at least this time she wasn't scrunched down on the floor. Nate introduced Lily to Elijah's wife, Olivia, though for the sake of keeping Lily and Nate hidden they couldn't look at one another.

The truck started to move down the road and Lily soon learned Elijah's wife was very friendly and much chattier than her taciturn husband. They made a series of turns over several minutes before finally slowing down and turning onto an obviously unpaved road.

"We're in the clear," Olivia called out. "I haven't seen anyone on the road behind us for a while. And we're on Morales ranch property now."

Lily and Nate cautiously sat up.

Through the front windshield Lily saw a sprawling ranch house with a few trees around it and a couple of motorcycles parked beneath the trees. The larger windows appeared darkly tinted, but lights glowed in the smaller windows.

Elijah parked by the front door. As they all got out of the truck, Olivia Morales reached over to wrap an arm around Lily's shoulders and give her a squeeze. "Welcome. I was in a dangerous situation when I first came to town. People here want to help you."

"Thank you." Right now she was open to all the help she could get.

"I arrived alone and scared and a certain deputy sheriff had his suspicions about me at first—" she looked pointedly at Nate "—but things ended up okay."

"I'm paid to be suspicious," Nate said blandly.

Olivia tucked a few strands of reddish-blond hair behind her ear and grinned at him.

They stepped into a large living room with comfortable-looking furniture and a huge fireplace at one end. A fire was burning, chasing away the outside chill. Lily was introduced to several people, including Elijah's parents, the owners of the property. She recognized some of the people in the room as riders with Vanquish the Darkness that she'd seen on the highway earlier today.

Something delicious involving barbecue sauce was cooking in the kitchen and her stomach growled. Turned out the s'mores weren't very substantial.

Lily spotted a couple of laptops on a low coffee table, the screens showing multiple sites on the ranch where security cameras had been set up.

"What is this place?" Despite Nate's description, Lily hadn't imagined anything like this. "Why do you need this kind of security?"

"We're a working cattle ranch," Elijah answered. "We're also members of a committed outreach program with some specialized experience." He glanced at Nate. "And some very helpful friends. Some people don't like that and we have to be able to keep an eye out for them."

"Oh." Lily didn't know what else to say. It was a little unnerving, but also comforting at the same time.

"Dinner will be ready in a half hour," Olivia said to Lily. "Let me show you to your room." Lily's bedroom was upstairs, and she was able to shower and change clothes before coming back downstairs for dinner.

After dinner, Elijah suggested Nate and Lily join him in a den off the living room to talk. Elijah's parents, Jonathan, Olivia and a young man named Bobby, who was introduced as their tech expert, would also be there.

Walking into the den, Lily noticed a couple of oil paintings of eagles on the wall. She sat down on a couch below the paintings. Nate sat next to her and for a moment her heart felt light in her chest. It felt good to be near him, but she reminded herself not to enjoy it too much. She might have renewed her conviction that ultimately God was in control of her life, but she still had a lot of hard work ahead of her when things went back to normal. She didn't have time for an elaborate social life. And Nate had his own life to get back to, anyway.

Nate stretched his arm up along the top of the couch behind her, which was almost like having him put his arm around her shoulders, and that lighthearted feeling threatened to turn into a mild panic. She didn't *want* to have this reaction to him. She'd been happily *unconnected* to any man before this nightmare started. And eating s'mores together didn't change anything. Even if it felt like it had.

"What exactly are we up against?" Elijah asked.

Lily and Nate each filled him in on what they knew.

"Tell me about Eddie Drake," Elijah said.

Lily described his physical appearance, including his slicked-back red hair. She clasped her hands in her lap. Talking about him made all the terrifying emotions come roaring back and her stomach started feeling knotted.

"He asked me out a few times," she continued. "Turning him down only seemed to encourage him to try harder. He bragged about himself, trying to impress me. It was annoying and I tuned it out." She looked up and Nate was watching her very intently. "The only specific thing I remember him saying was that he was into computers and technology and that he was really good at that stuff."

"There's an organized-crime element involved in what's going on with the cargo thefts and with Lily," Nate said. "We don't know the extent of it yet. But they could have sent out professionals to wrap things up and silence her."

Lily shivered as a chill passed through her. Professional killers might be after her. Nate took his arm from the back of the couch, dropped it down and held her hand.

"We can keep an eye out for any strangers coming onto the property," Bobby said, looking at the screen of the laptop balanced on his knees.

Lily looked down at her fingers entangled with Nate's. As time passed everything seemed to get murkier instead of clearer. With the people trying to kill her and with Nate.

Nate blew out a sigh. "I report back to work tomorrow. Maybe I'll learn something useful." He squeezed

Lily's hand and then let go of it. "You've had a long day. Why don't you get some rest?"

Her heart was beating so hard in her chest it was a moment before she could answer. "Good idea."

He stood and held out his hand. She took it and he pulled her to her feet. She vaguely noticed that her leg hurt, focusing instead on the steadying touch of his hand. She said good-night to everyone and he walked with her upstairs to the door of her room.

"I bet you're sorry you stopped at the Starlight Mart on your way back from Phoenix," Lily said from her doorway. She was afraid to let herself feel a connection with him, yet it was hard to let him go.

"Nah. I like to find trouble. That's why I do it for a living."

What he did for a living. That's right. All of his efforts were about doing his job. This wasn't about her.

"Well, I'm glad you did stop there." She tried to reel in her feelings for him, but it wasn't so easy.

He nodded. "We made it through another day. If we can keep doing that, we'll be fine."

"You're right." Another day, another battle to stay alive. "Good night." She stepped back into her room and softly closed the door.

Lily heard the low rumble of a motorcycle in the distance. She set down her pail and brushed the dirt off her gloved hands. After three days at the Morales ranch she was used to helping out with chores and she appreciated the chance to do something useful to earn her keep.

This afternoon she'd offered to help Olivia pack straw around some of the plants close to the barns and stables and behind the sprawling ranch house to help them survive the upcoming winter. She'd just returned to the small barn with Olivia to reload straw when she heard the sound of an engine.

Nate must be back. Ricky, reportedly the best auto mechanic in Oso County, was working on repairing Gaston's truck as fast as he could, but he'd needed to order some parts. In the meantime, Nate used a motor-cycle he kept at the Morales ranch to ride back and forth to work, bundling up to withstand the cold rush of air.

Lily quickly removed her glasses, used the tail of her flannel shirt to clean the lenses, patted her bangs to make sure they were lying flat and then smoothed the rest of her hair as best she could. When she put her glasses back on she realized Olivia was watching her and smiling.

Lily felt her cheeks burn. Could she have been any more obvious? And where had her silly reaction come from, anyway? She knew better. Yes, butterflies flut-tered in her stomach every time she was near Nate, but that didn't mean she had to turn off her brain. He stayed at the ranch because protecting her was part of his job. And she needed to get back to work herself as soon as she could.

Nate had put his hand atop hers the night they ar-rived at the ranch, sending a warm feeling of belonging through every cell in her body. But he hadn't touched her since. In fact, the very next day he'd saddled up and ridden out to work the ranch with Elijah, Elijah's dad and a cowboy named Mark. Jonathan and a couple members of Vanquish had stayed at the house to keep an eye on Lily.

He'd pulled away from her for a reason and he had

a right to that. He'd already poured a lot of energy into protecting her. She couldn't ask for more.

Did she want more from him?

The fluttering feeling in the pit of her stomach at the thought of seeing him again said yes. But that silly fluttering feeling had given her bad advice before. Following that advice had ultimately led her to the situation she was in right now. Fearing for her life. Fearing for her mother's safety.

Lily patted her jeans pocket, making sure her phone was still there. She'd been texting her mom and avoiding actual conversations. It was easier to withhold things that way, which was what Lily wanted to do right now. She didn't want her mom worrying.

But then it occurred to her that her mom might be doing the same thing. Would she tell Lily if her bronchitis was hanging on and she was getting sicker?

Maybe not.

That settled it. Lily needed to ignore those fluttery feelings about Nate and focus on things that mattered. It was selfish of her to even consider taking time for a relationship when she had a mess of a life to put back together.

She glanced at Olivia, wishing she could take back cleaning up and fixing her hair when she'd first heard Nate coming down the drive. Hopefully, Olivia wouldn't mention it to Nate. Maybe those flutters in Lily's heart would die down. If not, she'd figure out a way to stomp on them and kill them.

The sound of the motorcycle stopped. Nate must have parked it at the front of the house. Meanwhile, Elijah, his mom and Mark rode up on horseback. They'd been out for hours rounding up stray cattle and bringing them closer to the ranch buildings and their supplemental food supply before winter set in.

While the other riders headed for the stables to take care of their horses, Lily watched Elijah ride up close to Olivia and lean over. His wife, beaming, stood up on her tiptoes to meet his lips for a kiss.

Lily's heart ached a little.

She glanced back toward the house and saw Nate walking around the corner, the afternoon sunlight glinting off his sheriff's deputy badge. He wasn't alone. Sheriff Wolfsinger walked alongside him, as did Deputy Rios with Bubba trotting alongside her.

"They must have learned something," Elijah said to Lily. He got off his horse and reached for his wife's hand.

"Maybe it's good news," Lily said. "Maybe all of this is finally over."

After an exchange of greetings with the law officers, Elijah offered to leave. "If you need to talk in private, Olivia and I can bring Churchill to his stall and get him situated for the night."

The sheriff looked at him for a minute and then shook his head. "No. I think I can trust everybody here to keep their mouth shut." Elijah nodded. Wolfsinger glanced at Lily and Olivia and both women also nodded.

"There's still no sign of Eddie Drake," he said.

Lily's spirits sank. "Maybe he's fled the state?" she said hopefully.

"The cargo-theft task force met today. We learned some new information and maybe you can help us piece some things together." He focused his attention on Lily. "Nate said you told him Eddie was good with computers. What can you tell me about that?"

"Just that he *said* he was good with them. He boasted about all kinds of things." She thought for a minute, trying to remember any of the details from her typical workday that might be important. "He brought his own tablet and laptop to work. He had more than one phone. I got the impression he wanted to seem important, but now that I think of it I couldn't tell you exactly what he did at Torrent Trucking every day. I know he worked with routing a lot. He worked evenings and sometimes weekends."

"We've already talked to Bryan Torrent about obtaining access to Torrent Trucking computers and the company network. He's fine with that," Nate said. "Maybe our computer forensics people will be able to make some headway."

"I don't know that there's much of a company network," Lily said. "They used some truck-routing software and some accounting software, but everything I saw was pretty basic stuff you could buy online. None of it seemed very sophisticated, really."

"Maybe Bryan Torrent's business was pretty basic," Nate said. "But Eddie Drake might have been running something completely different under his nose."

"What do you mean?" Lily asked.

"Most cargo trailers, as well as the tractors, are set up to emit tracking signals," Nate explained to Olivia and Elijah. Then he turned back to Lily. "The task-force leaders said today that all of the thefts happened when tracking signals were turned off, or false location information was sent back to the owners' computers."

Lily shook her head. "I have to say Eddie doesn't seem smart enough to do something like that."

"He didn't have to invent the technology, he just had

to be willing to use it," Wolfsinger interjected. "Maybe that's the connection with organized crime. They paid for the programming and whatever else was required and put it into place."

"So you think Bryan Torrent might have been duped?" Lily asked.

"Mr. Torrent inherited the trucking company along with a couple of smaller businesses from his parents," Wolfsinger said. "He got into financial trouble and had to sell all of them except for Torrent Trucking. Sadly, his wife became very ill. After she passed away he used the insurance money to pay off his debts. According to him, he learned his lesson, accepted that he wasn't a good businessman and hired professionals who knew what they were doing to run his company."

"Speaking of people he hired, what can you tell us about Sheila?" Nate asked.

"Sheila? The dispatcher?" Lily shrugged. "You met her at the office. She's young. I never heard anyone complain about her at work. We didn't really have anything in common. Mostly she talked about going nightclubbing and I got the impression she and Eddie were friends and maybe hung out after work sometimes. Why?"

"She's gone missing," Nate said. "Her family is very worried."

ELEVEN

Lily had looked completely at home in her jeans and flannel shirt, with that little bit of straw in her hair. Making the drive from downtown Painted Rock out to the Morales ranch, Nate kept that image of her fixed in his mind while his eyes were on the road.

Ricky the mechanic had called to say he'd finished the repairs to Gaston's truck just after Sheriff Wolfsinger and Deputy Rios left the Morales ranch. Elijah had given Nate a ride into town to the mechanic's garage and was following him back to the ranch.

Nate rubbed his eyes and tried to dismiss his mental image of Lily as a ranch woman. She was getting to him and he needed to do something about that. Maybe he should move back into his apartment. He was still assigned to the Painted Rock substation, but he hoped his recent work in Phoenix plus his assignment to the cargo-theft task force might get him transferred back to Copper Mesa. The Morales family and their Vanquish friends were perfectly capable of protecting Lily. Maybe things would start to go his way and whoever had shot at him and Lily would break into Nate's apartment looking for her while Nate was there. He would love to meet that guy.

More troubling at the moment was the fact that Sheila, the dispatcher from Torrent Trucking, was missing and Nate feared the worst. Yes, there was a chance she'd simply taken a trip because she felt like getting out of town. Or she could be part of the cargo-theft ring and had hightailed it out of Copper Mesa because it looked as if the operation was falling apart and she was in danger of getting caught.

But maybe professional killers were in town and they'd grabbed her. Or maybe Eddie Drake had snapped and done something terrible to her. What if they now had Lily in their sights? If someone was determined enough and had the resources—someone like a professional hitman—they could get to her on the Morales ranch. The thought made Nate's stomach clench. He couldn't leave Lily's protection up to someone else. He had to take care of her himself.

Nate pressed down on the gas pedal, picking up speed. He could call Lily to see if she was okay, but what he really wanted was to see her. He hadn't even been gone that long, but he needed to know with absolute certainty that she was all right.

Nate reminded himself he didn't have any kind of claim on her. Not as a friend or anything else. He was a cop. She was a woman who needed protection. They'd had a friend in common back in their teenage years, and in honor of Joseph Suh he would keep her safe. That was it.

No, that wasn't it. But that *should* be it. That should put the stop to anything personal happening between them. He'd promised himself he would never risk putting a woman in the same situation his mom had been in, leaving her widowed and feeling abandoned. Nate didn't go to work every morning thinking that day would be his last, but the risk was there.

His entire life and his sense of purpose were wrapped up in being a lawman. It wasn't just a job for him and it wasn't something he could quit. Not now. Maybe one day, when he was older, he'd be ready to turn in his badge and help run the Blue Spruce. But not yet.

It was the undeniable truth that he didn't have the background to make a good family man. He'd learned a lot from Bud and Ellen and his interactions with the Suh family, but those early years had been a chaotic mess. He had a general idea of how parents were supposed to interact with small children, but there was still so much left that was a mystery to him.

For a moment, that image of Lily on a ranch was back in his mind. And she was walking around with a couple of little kids following behind her. She'd mentioned she wanted to have children one day.

Nate shook his head. "Stop it."

Anger at himself flared hot across the surface of his skin. He should never have moved into the Morales house. He should have stayed in his own apartment. Moving back into the apartment and living alone again once Lily was safe was going to feel much colder than it had felt before.

But he would adjust. Just like he'd adjusted when he first moved out here from Copper Mesa. And if he had any character at all, he would keep his feelings for Lily to himself.

He turned onto the drive leading up to the Morales ranch, parked by the front door and got out of the truck.

Elijah parked his truck, got out, and walked up the front steps beside Nate. "Good thing there wasn't a cop around." He slapped a hand on Nate's shoulder and gave him a hearty squeeze. "You might have gotten a speeding ticket."

Nate managed a small laugh but he didn't slow down as he headed for the front door. When the time was right, he'd start keeping his distance from Lily. Right now he just needed to see her and make sure she was okay.

As soon as he opened the door he smelled butter-pecan tarts. Lily liked to bake. She'd made something every day since the day after they'd arrived at the ranch. Nate headed for the kitchen.

He found her there.

Strands of dark hair had come loose from her pony-tail. She had flour smudges on her cheeks and on the black frames of her glasses. She was moving in front of the stove, favoring her injured leg.

She turned to him and her brown eyes looked so soft and inviting that for a few seconds he simply took comfort in gazing into them. For the moment it felt like every worry he had in the world had been wrapped up in making sure that she was okay. And now that he finally saw for himself that she was fine, a rare feeling of peace settled over him.

"These butter-pecan tarts are awesome." Bobby, the curly-haired tech expert for Vanquish the Darkness, was the only other person in the kitchen. He sat at a small table, helping himself to another tart. Nate hadn't even noticed him until now.

"They smell good," Nate said quietly. His attention was back on Lily and she'd locked gazes with him.

"Gaston will be happy to hear his truck has been repaired," Lily said.

Nate shrugged a shoulder. "I'll wait until tomorrow to tell him. Make him suffer a little longer. Builds character."

She laughed and reached up to tuck a stray hair behind her ear.

Nate heard the scrape of a chair and from the corner of his eye he saw Bobby get up and leave, taking several tarts with him.

And it wasn't hard to guess why he'd scooted out so fast.

Nate's feelings for Lily were probably written all over his face. And the way she was gazing at him and fidgeting a little bit nervously made him think she might be feeling something, too.

Stop. If Nate was truly a man of character, he would stop what was going on between them right now. Lily wanted a family one day. She'd said so. And he was not a family man. No matter how much he might want to be one.

"Having that truck repaired is one less problem to worry about." Nate consciously made the effort to change the expression on his face and in his eyes, trying to look like he did when he was working. Closed-off. Unemotional. Detached.

Lily looked away and he felt the sudden break of connection between them like a sharp physical sting.

He felt like a jerk, but it was the right thing to do.

A few seconds later she turned back to him and

crossed her arms over her chest. He'd expected hurt or sorrow in her eyes. Instead, she saw fire. "Speaking of worries, I'm about to create a big one for you," she said crisply.

Uh-oh. "And what's that going to be?"

"I need to go see my mom."

Nate shook his head. "No."

She squared her shoulders. "Look, I'm not careless and I'm not an idiot. But my mom's been sick and I need to see for myself that she's okay. I haven't exactly been telling her the complete truth lately and I think she might be doing the same thing with me."

Nate crossed his arms over his chest, matching her stubborn stance. "Let's wait a few days."

"I've already been up here for a few days. There's no sign the bad guys know I'm here. We can rent or borrow a car that's not connected with me in any way. I can hide in the back or wear a disguise. We can take Vanquish riders with us if you want to. Or if you think that will draw too much attention, we won't. And if you don't want anything to do with it, I understand. I can figure out a way to make the trip without you."

She had really thought this through. And if there was one thing he'd learned about Lily Doyle, she wasn't a quitter. She wouldn't back down.

It looked as if he was going back to Copper Mesa. Because until this was finished, she wasn't going anywhere without him.

"Looking at mug shots and *not* recognizing any of the faces still gives us valuable information," Nate said to Lily. "It helps us narrow our focus."

That was good to hear, because she was beginning to feel as if she'd let everybody down.

She and Nate were standing with Sheriff Wolfsinger in the squad room of the sheriff's department in Copper Mesa.

"Nate's right," Sheriff Wolfsinger said. "You've been helpful. Thank you for coming in."

"You're welcome."

The sheriff nodded, then turned and headed back toward his office. He was a busy man, yet he always managed to make her feel as if he didn't begrudge the time spent with her.

When Nate had called to tell Sheriff Wolfsinger he wanted to use a vacation day and take Lily to visit her mom, the sheriff had told him to consider it a workday, but to dress in casual clothes to better help Lily fade into the landscape. And then he'd told Nate to bring Lily by his office. He'd assigned a detective to thoroughly investigate Torrent Trucking and the detective had collected pictures of known criminals that had passed through the trucking facility. Sheriff Wolfsinger wanted Lily to take a look at them and see if anyone seemed familiar. Unfortunately, no one had.

He'd also asked a few questions about Sheila, but Lily couldn't provide much information about her, either. Sheila worked in a different office from Lily and while they'd passed the time chatting now and then, they'd never had any deep conversations or talked much about their personal lives. If Sheila was involved in any criminal activity, she'd hidden it well.

"Don't worry, we'll get 'em eventually." Deputy Rios walked into the squad room with Bubba at her side. The loyal K-9's ears were tilted forward as though he didn't intend to miss a single word anyone said.

"Criminals get greedy and rat each other out. Or they get impatient or lazy," Rios added. "Even the smart ones. Then we get 'em."

"I know everybody's working hard on this," Lily said to her. "I just hope Eddie Drake or somebody else involved with all this makes a mistake soon."

"Hang in there." Rios gave her arm an encouraging squeeze. Then she turned to Nate. "Bubba and I are headed back to Painted Rock. See you later."

"Looks like we're done here. Let's go check on your mom," Nate said. "See how she and those furry little big-nosed mosquitoes she calls dogs are getting along."

Lily knew he was trying to cheer her up. She tried to smile, but couldn't. "Let's swing by Ruby's Plant and Pottery Shop. I know Scott is out of the hospital. I'd like to stop by and see how things are going."

Nate raised his eyebrows slightly. "All things considered, they might prefer you didn't."

"You're right. They probably don't ever want to see me again." Lily felt her shoulders drop. "I bet I don't have my catering job anymore, either. Who would want to be anywhere near me?" She sounded like a petulant twelve-year-old but she didn't care. After a series of stupid decisions she'd finally gotten some traction putting her life together, made some headway toward not being a financial burden on her mom. And now this. She'd nearly gotten killed, she'd likely lost all of her jobs and other people had gotten hurt because of her.

Vaguely, she remembered her recent decision to stop

trying to control every single thing. To trust God. But that was really hard to do.

Nate led the way, heading out a side door of the sheriff's department and toward the truck he had borrowed from the Morales ranch. Elijah had looked slightly pained as he'd handed over the keys to his shiny black truck while his wife grinned beside him, reassuring her husband that he could drive her small sedan anytime he wanted.

Nate took Lily's arm and seemed to be looking every direction at once as they walked to Elijah's truck. She tried not to think too much about the comforting feel of his muscles.

"I should have bought a wig," she joked grimly as they got into the truck. Nate had been trying to lighten up things a couple of minutes ago. She should try, too.

She'd been pleasantly surprised when he'd agreed to this trip into town. Elijah had suggested gathering some of the riders from Vanquish to come with them, but Nate had quickly shot that down as a bad idea. Deputy Rios had insisted she follow at a discreet distance behind them as they drove to Copper Mesa and wouldn't take no for an answer. Wolfsinger had decided to keep Rios in Painted Rock even though Nate had returned to work, just so there'd be an extra deputy in the area if someone found out Lily was at the Morales ranch and came after her.

Inside the truck Nate gave Lily a long look and she thought he might actually be considering a trip to a wig shop. Then he started rooting around, first in the front seat and then in the back, until he finally found a baseball cap. It looked like something Jonathan would wear. "Put this on," he said. "And tuck your hair underneath it."

She did as he asked and he nodded approvingly. "You look different with your hair up. That should make it harder for anyone to recognize you. While we're driving around in town we need to be extra careful."

Lily flipped down a visor mirror and looked at her reflection. The cap was not a flattering look for her.

"Those black rims on your glasses are distinctive, too." Nate turned the key and the truck engine rumbled to life. "Maybe you should take them off."

And ride around town with everything a blur? "I think I'll keep them on."

"Okay."

They'd talked about this part of the trip before leaving Painted Rock. That they might not be so noticeable on the highway, but driving around town was a different story. Someone could glance over from the next lane or from the sidewalk and recognize Lily. Or Nate.

Eddie Drake had not been seen or heard from since Lily talked to him on the phone. There was some discussion at the sheriff's department that the missing Sheila might be with him. Maybe they had left town together. Or maybe they were still here in Copper Mesa looking for Lily, waiting for her to become impatient and show her face in town.

Maybe this trip was a mistake.

Lily flipped up the collar on her jacket and slid down in her seat. Why couldn't these criminals leave her alone? She hadn't heard or seen anything significant. If there had been any illegal activities going on around her at Torrent Trucking she'd been oblivious.

"Why did they even hire me?" she asked, voicing the question that had just popped into her head.

"Huh?" Nate glanced over at her.

"At Torrent Trucking. If something criminal was going on, something secret, why did they even hire me to begin with?"

"It could be that not everyone there is involved in the criminal activity."

"So Mr. Torrent might really be innocent?"

Nate shrugged. "Maybe they want some noncriminals around to maintain the appearance that the business is legit."

Lily's thoughts took a dark turn. "What if Sheila is one of the noncriminals and now somebody's afraid she may have seen or overheard something, too? What if they've done something to her?"

Nate's jaw muscles tensed and he was quiet for a few seconds. "Let's hope that's not the case," he finally said.

They headed for Penny's house, but instead of taking the straightest, fastest route Nate looped around a few times. He'd randomly make a series of right or left turns, which would take them back to where they'd just been. Lily tried to stay vigilant and look around like Nate did, but if she saw the same car behind them after a loop—a sign that they were being followed—she wouldn't know. Memorizing all the cars she saw as they passed through downtown Copper Mesa turned out to be a talent she just didn't possess.

Watching Nate concentrate so hard on looking out for her, Lily felt appreciation for all he'd done for her tug at her heart. Okay, it was probably something more than appreciation. She tried to make the feeling go away, but she couldn't. Sitting here in the truck, close to him, she started to feel that sense of connection she'd felt for a few moments in his apartment and in the Morales kitchen last night.

Maybe she didn't want to resist the feeling anymore. Maybe she wanted to see where it would lead.

Maybe that would be another big mistake.

They reached Penny's house. After taking a good look around, Nate let her get out of the truck and walk inside.

Abigail and Beatrice barked in happy hysteria when they saw Lily. Nate moved stiffly around them, as if terrified he'd step on one of the little dogs.

Lily's mom came over and gave her a hug. Her lungs still made a slight whistling sound when she breathed and she looked pale, but she didn't seem nearly as bad as Lily had imagined.

"You look well," Lily's mom said, giving her daughter a quick visual assessment. "When you called and said you were coming by I was worried something else had gone wrong."

A pang of guilt squeezed the center of Lily's body. Her mom had enough going on health-wise without having to worry so much about Lily. She would withhold the details of some of the more terrifying things that had happened to her for a little while longer.

They settled onto a couch while Penny went to make tea.

Lily's mom smiled at Lily and glanced at the top of her head. "Nice hat. Have you joined a baseball team?"

Lily touched it, then grinned as she pulled off the baseball cap and let her hair fall down to her shoulders.

Seeing her mom smiling despite everything reminded her she came from tough stock. Doyle women were survivors. Not just survivors. *Fighters.* They might get knocked down, but they got back up.

She glanced at Nate, wondering if he'd noticed that was true about her despite her occasional moments of fear and hopelessness.

Penny came back with tea and they sat and talked for a little while. Beatrice climbed up into Nate's lap and let him pet her. Abby stubbornly sat on the floor and eyeballed Nate.

"Let's go by the Blue Spruce," Lily said to Nate when they walked out of Penny's house fifteen minutes later. "We can check on Bud and Ellen."

"I'm sure they're fine," Nate said distractedly as he looked up and down the street. When they got to the truck he opened her door for her. "Gaston would tell me if there was anything to worry about."

"Well, they might want to check on *you* and make sure you're okay." She climbed up into the seat, flipped down the visor mirror and tucked her hair back up under the baseball cap. "We're already this close to the ranch," she continued after Nate got in and shut his door. "We're in a truck no one would connect with either one of us. At the rate things are going, who knows how long it'll be before it's safe for us to come back this way again?"

Nate didn't say anything as he pulled away from the curb and steered the truck toward the highway. When he got to the intersection where he had to make a turn, he hesitated.

"Come on," Lily said. "You know you want to check on them."

"You're relentless," he finally muttered. And then he made the turn that would take them to the Blue Spruce Ranch.

TWELVE

Nate parked in front of the house at the Blue Spruce Ranch, got out of the truck and took a deep breath of cool, crisp air. He glanced up. Clouds had rolled in, bringing a gentle flurry of snow with them.

His moment of peace came to an abrupt end when Gaston strode over to him from the stables, red-faced.

"Your truck is fine." Nate held up his hands in a placating gesture before Gaston could open his mouth. "I got it back from the mechanic yesterday. It's better than new. And it's definitely a lot cleaner than it was when you lent it to me. The only reason I'm driving Elijah's truck right now is because Lily and I didn't want to be easily identified."

Speaking of which, he turned toward Lily and watched her slide out of the truck. She'd taken a couple of minutes to ditch the baseball cap, brush her dark hair and put on some lip gloss. She looked gorgeous.

Whoa. It didn't matter how she looked. And Nate needed to get a grip. *Now.*

The front door of the house swung open and Bud and Ellen walked out to greet them. Gaston, still red-faced, flexed his jaw muscles. He looked as if he had something to say, but was struggling to keep his trap shut.

After Bud and Ellen finished with hugs and pats on the back, Ellen turned to Lily. "You must be hungry. Let me get you something to eat."

"That sounds good," Lily answered.

Nate thought it sounded good, too.

"I'll put on a pot of coffee, too," Ellen added, crossing her arms over her chest and shivering a little. "I've got some chicken salad and fresh rolls for sandwiches." She tilted her head toward the house. "Come on. Let's get inside."

As soon as the door shut behind them, Gaston finally spoke. "You shouldn't have brought Lily here. We've had somebody on the property today. Not near the house, but on the road. I don't know who it is. It might be someone looking for you and Lily."

"Maybe it's just kids," Nate countered, not wanting to fan the flames of panic. The Blue Spruce had some very scenic spots. Waterfalls, ponds, small canyons. People sometimes came up to have a look around. Adults usually asked for permission. Teenagers didn't.

"That's possible," Gaston said as he, Bud and Nate moved toward a corner of the long front porch, where they were sheltered from the snow flurry. "But it's also possible it's some idiot looking for you and Lily."

"Maybe it's Eddie Drake," Nate said, thinking out loud. "Or his criminal bosses." A ripple of fear passed through him before hardening into frustration. He turned his gaze from Gaston to Bud and then back to Gaston again. "Why didn't you tell me about this sooner?"

"Why didn't you tell us you were coming back to

the ranch?" Gaston snapped back. "And by that I mean doing something other than what you did. Waiting to call until you were just a couple of miles down the road with Lily beside you so she'd likely hear anything I said." Gaston shook his head. "What were you thinking?"

"There's no reason to hide the truth from Lily. She can take it."

It was true. At her core, Lily was rock-solid. Nate stayed focused on that realization for a few seconds, then he wrenched his thoughts away from her and glanced toward the ranch house. "Are you keeping this a secret from Ellen, too?"

"Oh, no." Bud emphatically shook his head. "I wouldn't keep anything like that from her." He exchanged glances with Gaston. "It didn't seem wise to mention it in front of Lily before we talked to you. We meant no disrespect to her, we just didn't know if her nerves were shot after all she's been through. And nobody would blame her if that was the case."

"Did you call the deputy assigned to this area?" Nate asked.

"Not yet," Gaston said impatiently. "I called *you* first. Check your voice mail." He exchanged glances with Bud and then turned back to Nate. "We had no idea you and Lily would show up out here without warning us ahead of time."

Nate's phone rang. It was Sheriff Wolfsinger.

"Where are you?" the sheriff asked without preamble. Nate told him.

"We found Torrent's dispatcher, Sheila," Wolfsinger said.

"Alive?" Nate held his breath.

"No." The sheriff sighed. "She was shot and thrown down a ravine."

"Where?" Nate asked, dreading to hear that she'd been found somewhere on the Blue Spruce Ranch. Maybe that's why the stranger was out here. He glanced up toward the high ridges on the property, looking for a human silhouette. But the clouds had dropped down low and his view was blocked.

The sheriff described a location a good twenty miles away back in the direction of Torrent Trucking and the Starlight Mart. While Wolfsinger was talking, Nate walked into the house looking for Lily.

"We don't know if Eddie Drake killed Sheila or if it was somebody else," the sheriff added. "But it looks like somebody's getting desperate again."

Nate told him about the car that had driven by the ranch. Wolfsinger said he'd have the deputy assigned to the area drive up to the ranch house and stay there to protect Nate's family.

"Lily and I will be out of here and headed back to Painted Rock in just a few minutes," Nate said.

"Good." The sheriff disconnected.

Nate found Lily sitting on a stool at the cooking island in the kitchen eating a chicken salad sandwich and chatting with Ellen. "We've got to go. *Now.*"

Nate told her about the unknown person who had apparently driven out to the ranch. And then he told her about Sheila.

The smile dropped from Lily's lips and the color drained from her face. She set her sandwich back on her plate.

Ellen quickly wrapped the uneaten sandwich and put it, along with some chips and homemade cookies, into a bag. She grabbed a couple of water bottles from the fridge and as soon as Lily slid her arms into her jacket Ellen shoved the bag of food at her.

After Lily took the bag, Ellen gave her a hug. Then Ellen gave Nate a hug, too, lingering a few seconds longer than she normally did. As they headed to the front door, Nate told Ellen a deputy was coming to the ranch house to keep an eye on things.

He and Lily got into the truck and hustled out of there. Fortunately, as they headed down toward Copper Mesa, the snow flurries lightened and finally stopped. That meant Nate could drive just a little bit faster, and he did.

His mind was racing as he made the turn that would take him toward the Starlight Mart and the intersection with the road to Painted Rock. Maybe it wasn't Eddie Drake that murdered Sheila. It could have been some random psychopath or someone from her life that Nate had no way of knowing about. Whoever had been out on the Blue Spruce property might not have any connection with Lily or Torrent Trucking or the cargo thefts. Maybe this was all a coincidence.

But Nate didn't believe in coincidences. For the moment he had to assume someone was desperate and getting organized. And that person, or those persons, might be after Lily or Nate or anyone connected to them.

As they neared the Starlight Mart, he glanced at Lily. She gave him a wan smile that made his heart ache. He took the turn north toward Painted Rock and floored it.

Part of him wanted to take her to the Morales ranch and then head right back to the Blue Spruce to do some tracking. If anybody was out there, he'd find them.

Maybe he could find out exactly what was going on and who was behind it all. Then he could bring an end to it.

But there was also a part of him that didn't dare leave Lily at the Morales ranch without staying with her. Elijah Morales was good. There were other members of Vanquish the Darkness with military and police skills. But Nate knew for a fact that they didn't have as much heart in the fight to protect Lily as he did.

Of course, he had the backing of the sheriff's department, but they couldn't be everywhere at once. If he called them for help it would take time for them to respond. He needed to be prepared for anything. Which meant he needed some of the extra equipment he kept at his apartment. In particular he was thinking of a bulletproof vest for Lily. Just in case someone tracked them to the Morales ranch.

"I was engaged to a man who became involved with another woman," Lily said after they'd been driving for a while.

What? Nate felt a quick flash of fear. Why did she want to talk about that *now*? He wasn't good at these emotional kinds of conversations under the best of circumstances. And right now he had way too many things on his mind to figure out what to say. Or, just as importantly, what *not* to say.

"The guy was an idiot," Nate finally said, going with his gut reaction. "He was a fool."

Lily was quiet for a while. Okay, good. That was over with. Nate breathed out a sigh of relief. Now they could get back to focusing on the here-and-now problems they needed to deal with.

"After years of keeping my nose to the grindstone, I decided I was going to let myself live a little," Lily continued doggedly. "And that led to a whole series of bad decisions."

Oh, no, she was back at it.

"So your life got off track a little," Nate said. "That happens."

"It got off track *a lot*."

He already knew most of this. Why was she bringing it up again? And why now?

They reached the outskirts of Painted Rock.

"The thing is, when I think about my life and the reality that it could end at any moment, I realize how much time I've wasted wallowing in regret," Lily said. "And now I'm finished with doing that."

Nate felt himself grin.

"That wasn't supposed to be funny," she grumbled.

"I'm just happy for you." He never knew what Lily Doyle was going to say, but it was always interesting. And every now and then there were moments, and this was one of them, when he felt that connection with her. Because he knew exactly what she was going through. When his life was in danger, he found himself focusing on the important stuff and ditching everything else, as well.

"Once all of this is over, I'm going to work really hard," she said, her voice taking an optimistic tone. "Start my own business. Maybe a café. Something food-related."

At least now she was focused on her future instead of her past. Or the danger that was dogging her. That was good.

She had dreams and Nate was happy to know that.

"What about you?" she asked. "What are you going

to do when whoever is behind all this trouble is brought to justice and our lives go back to normal?"

He could feel her looking at him and sensed her unspoken question. *Did they have a future together?* No. Yes. Maybe. He couldn't think about that right now. He had more practical things to focus on.

"I'll go back to doing what I do best," he muttered. "Catching bad guys."

"That's it?" she asked, her voice now sounding flat.

"And maybe some ranching."

That was enough to make him happy. At least it had been before he ran into Lily at the Starlight Mart. He couldn't resist stealing a glance at her. She was staring at the road ahead, pensive. The woman had courage. He'd seen it. And it was enough to make him question the depth of his own courage. He'd thought avoiding a deeper personal relationship with her was the better and wiser decision on his part. Now he wasn't so sure.

"Plenty of people grow up in dysfunctional families, but they don't use that as an excuse to hide from what they truly want," she said.

"And you assume I want you?" he snapped in response. This conversation was getting too personal too fast. She needed to back off.

"I think you want more for your life than just work," she said mildly. "And why is that so terrible?"

Because he was already closer to her than he'd meant to be. Already too used to seeing her every day. What if he messed things up? What if he ruined things? What if he was a disappointment to people who loved him, just like his mom was?

He cleared his throat. "I'm going to take you to the

Morales ranch and then I'll swing by my apartment to grab some things."

"Why don't we just stop on the way?" Her tone had become polite and distant. It felt as if the temperature in the cab of the truck had dropped a couple of degrees.

Well, good. That's what he'd wanted, right? "Okay," he said. "I'll make it quick."

They rolled into downtown Painted Rock and Nate turned from Stagecoach Road, the main drag through town, onto a side street. He drove over the bridge that crossed the small stream winding through town and then passed the city park. Houses and alleyways fanned out behind the businesses.

Nate's apartment was on the corner at the end of the street. Four separate buildings formed a hacienda-like square, with meandering pathways between them that were lush with evergreen vegetation.

"Hold on a second." Nate parked the truck, got out and looked around. Apparently satisfied, he opened Lily's door and reached for her arm. "Stay close to me."

Lily couldn't help feeling the warm sensation of comfort and strength that raced across the surface of her skin when he touched her. And that feeling reminded her that she wanted more from him than he was willing to give. She was mad at him. And mad at herself.

They walked along a pathway to his front door and he slid his key into the lock.

Lily heard a ragged intake of breath behind her and turned. A dirty, disheveled human form sprang out from behind a cluster of bushes. It was Eddie Drake. "Nate!"

Nate whirled around and let go of her arm just as a flash of metal arced downward.

A tire iron clanked to the ground and Lily felt herself being jerked backward. She flailed her arms, but Eddie had gripped her zipped-up coat by the collar and she couldn't break free.

Nate moved to reach for her and then froze, his arms stretched toward her.

For the third time in less than a month, Lily had a gun pressed to the side of her neck. It was a sickeningly familiar feeling. The buoyant hope she'd felt about her future just minutes ago crumbled like cold ashes. Maybe all of her efforts to stay alive were pointless. Maybe getting shot was how her life was supposed to end.

Eddie snaked his arm across the base of her neck, pulling her closer to him. He was breathing hard and he reeked of stale, sour sweat. His red hair fell around his face in greasy, dusty ringlets.

Nate slowly lowered his right arm toward his hip, where Lily knew he kept a gun under his coat.

"I've got nothing to lose, Deputy," Eddie said in a soft voice that made Lily's skin crawl. He pressed his gun into her skin a little harder. "You'd better think carefully about what you're going to do."

From the corner of her eye Lily saw drapes flutter in the window of the apartment next door. *Please let the neighbor call for help.*

Eddie started backing up, dragging Lily with him.

Nate stared in her direction, but he wasn't looking at Lily. He was watching Eddie, with that cold, calculating cop expression in his eyes.

"Eddie, let me go." Lily commanded herself to speak in a soothing tone, though her voice wavered a little. Maybe if she calmed Eddie down she could get him to act like a normal, sane human being. But then maybe he didn't even have control over his actions anymore. Maybe he'd already snapped once before and murdered Sheila.

"Eddie, please."

"*Now* you want to talk to me?" As he spoke, his gaze was still locked on Nate. He continued to move backward, pulling Lily with him. "Funny, you weren't so interested in talking to me before."

She forced herself to seem calm even though her heart hammered so hard in her chest she could barely take a breath. "Eddie, I don't know what's going on, but you don't have to do this."

He stumbled but quickly regained his footing. He must have been on the run the last few days. Law enforcement all over the state had been on the lookout for him. He probably hadn't gotten much rest. Most likely he hadn't eaten well if he'd even eaten at all. Maybe he was getting weaker and that would give Lily her chance to escape.

Or it might make him more likely to panic and pull the trigger on that handgun.

"Don't worry," he said, still pulling Lily backward with him, still holding her tight against his foul-smelling clothes. "We'll have plenty of time to talk when we're alone."

She felt a tear escape and roll down her face. She didn't want him to see her despair, but she couldn't help it.

"If you try to follow us," Eddie called out to Nate, "I'll kill her."

He was taking her toward a small parking lot at the side of the apartment complex. She could hear a car engine idling. Her blood ran cold. What if there wasn't really anywhere he wanted to take her? What if he was just going to shoot her in the parking lot and then speed away?

Fueled by panic, she tried to twist out of his grasp, but his hold was too tight and he nearly broke her arm. "Try that again," he whispered in her ear, "and I'll go back and shoot your cop sweetheart before I shoot you."

They reached the car and he shoved her in on the passenger side. Then, gun still pointed at her, he forced her to climb over to the driver's side while he got into the passenger seat.

He slammed the car door shut. "We're leaving town. Start driving, nice and easy. Don't do anything stupid."

Lily put the car into gear and very slowly drove out of the parking lot and onto the street.

People were bundled up and walking in the neighborhood despite the cold weather. A couple of kids and a dog were playing by the little white gazebo in the small park. Life still went on even though Lily's world was coming to an end.

She thought about shoving open the car door and trying to run away. She also thought about trying to grab his gun as he glanced back in the direction where they'd left Nate. But with each of those impulses she imagined a stray shot being fired and something horrible happening to an innocent bystander. Maybe even one of those kids.

With a heavy heart she kept driving forward. She'd only gone a little ways down the street when an Oso County sheriff's department patrol car pulled forward on a cross street ahead of her and stopped in the middle of the road. She hit the brakes.

"I said drive!" Eddie screamed. He'd turned around to look out the back window again, like he was afraid Nate might be following them.

"I can't," Lily shouted back.

Eddie turned and saw the cop car blocking their path. He cursed. Agitated, he started taking rapid breaths. He moved around in his seat, looking in every direction. And then he shoved his gun against Lily's temple.

This was it. He was going to kill her now. He'd already said he had nothing to lose. *Dear Lord*, Lily prayed, glancing at the kids and the dog in the park. *Please don't let anyone else get hurt.*

THIRTEEN

"No!" Nate punched the steering wheel of the truck when he saw a second sheriff's department patrol car pull into the intersection behind Eddie's car, boxing in the desperate criminal with Lily trapped inside the vehicle beside him.

After Eddie grabbed Lily, Nate had raced to the truck in the parking lot, intending to follow them at a discreet distance. Drake was obviously on the edge of sanity, maybe even past the edge, and any fast approach, any confrontation, could feel like a threat and push him to lash out with Lily right there within his reach.

Nate's hasty plan had been to follow them wherever they were going, hoping Eddie didn't recognize him in the truck and that the dusky early evening light would make his appearance less obvious.

Nate had quickly come to the grim conclusion that Eddie's likely endgame was to kill Lily and escape. But he'd have to take her somewhere to finish his plan and Nate meant to follow him there and surprise him. He'd already planned to alert Sheriff Wolfsinger in hopes of avoiding an interaction with a patrol car should a deputy recognize Eddie. The last thing Nate wanted was any action that might escalate the already tense situation.

A blue light slowly began to rotate on the light bar atop the cop car in front of Eddie and Lily. The loudspeaker clicked on, carrying the voice of Deputy Crystal Rios. "Passenger, step out of the car with your hands up."

Somebody must have seen Eddie forcing Lily into the car and called it in. Deputy Rios might not have recognized Eddie, or realized Lily was in the car with him, until she'd already attempted the stop.

Things could go sideways fast. Nate needed a new plan.

He slammed the truck into Park, grabbed his gun, got out and started running. Lily and Eddie were only a couple blocks away. If Eddie was distracted by the cops, maybe Nate could surprise him if he snuck up on foot.

He headed toward Eddie's car, sticking to the edge of the road, where the trees and bushes surrounding the small community park gave him cover. He slowed down when he got closer, moving a little farther off the road and pressing into the foliage. He crouched down to make himself less obvious for those last few steps.

The streetlights buzzed to life. Old-style pole lights, chosen to maintain the historic feel townspeople loved so much, cast pools of light down the darkening street. Thanks to their help, Nate could see through the back windshield inside the car. He rose up slightly. Through the gap between the front seats he could see Lily's profile. She sat facing forward, her shoulders rigid, chin lifted. If she could maintain that composure he'd seen her exhibit before in life-threatening situations, it might save her life.

Sitting beside her in the car, Eddie turned back and forth, looking at Lily to his left, then Deputy Rios's car in front and then back to Lily again. His gun was out of sight. It could be trained on Rios or on Lily.

Obviously agitated, Eddie began to shift around even more restlessly in the car. Not a good time to put added pressure on him. So far Rios was giving him some breathing room. Good call.

Nate eased a few more steps down the street, then stopped, hoping to stay out of Eddie's line of sight if he turned around or looked in his car's side mirrors.

Nate hit the speed-dial number for Rios on his phone. She might not answer. She might not even know Nate was there.

"I see you," the deputy said tersely when she picked up after the third ring. She was on speaker, her face was turned toward Eddie's car, but her phone was out of sight. Eddie probably wouldn't be able to see that she was talking to someone.

Nate told her what had just happened.

"I thought we might be dealing with Eddie Drake when the call came in, given the location where the abduction took place, but I couldn't know for certain until I got here," she said. "Sheriff Wolfsinger's on his way up here from Copper Mesa. Meanwhile we're keeping things as calm and easy as we can."

The patrol car behind Eddie and Lily pulled slightly forward. Unfortunately, Eddie must have seen it. He screamed something at Lily, though Nate couldn't discern the words. He saw her shoulders raise up protectively and her head drop down. And then he saw the gun. Eddie had lifted it up into plain view. And, of course, it was pointed at Lily.

Nate's stomach clenched and his heart hammered so hard in his chest he could feel it in the base of his throat. *Oh, dear Lord.*

He drew in a breath and cleared his mind of every thought except for what was happening at this very moment. Imagining how terrified Lily felt or dwelling on the realization of how much he cared for her would not help, though that was the direction his thoughts wanted to go.

Adrenaline made his hands tremble slightly as he gripped his gun tighter and slowly stood up, setting his sights on Eddie.

He glanced around to make certain there were no innocent bystanders in his potential line of fire. The sidewalks were clear. The park was likewise empty. An alert adult had gathered the kids and the dog who were playing in the grass and ushered them out the park's back entrance.

Rios turned off the bar lights on the roof of her cruiser. "We don't want to hurt you," she called out over her loudspeaker. "Let's talk."

Nate could see Eddie shoving at Lily with his free hand, his other hand still holding the gun pressed into the side of her head. She rolled down her window. "No talking!" she called out, her voice breaking. "Just let us go!"

"You know I can't do that," Rios answered. "Both of you get out of the car and we'll talk."

Nate took another couple of steps forward, hoping Deputy Rios would keep Eddie distracted until he could get close enough for a clean shot. Eddie must have murdered Sheila. That was why he'd snapped. Something had driven him too far, whether it was his organized crime bosses or his own greed. He'd obviously gone beyond rational behavior and there was nothing to stop him from killing Lily. It wasn't just an idle threat when he'd said he had nothing to lose.

The passenger door flew open and Eddie slid out, dragging Lily with him. When she first tried to stand, her knees buckled. He yanked her back to her feet.

The street they were on was the next one over from Stagecoach Road, the shopping and dining hub for Painted Rock. There was a store-lined passageway between the two streets, forming an arcade. Eddie headed in that direction dragging Lily with him.

Rios got out of her car, gun drawn and speaking into her collar mic. She started after them.

A couple of patrol cars pulled forward from a side street and waited. With no further reason to stay out of sight, Nate took off running after Rios. Behind him, he could hear Bubba barking and whining in the back of Rios's patrol car.

The arcade had been pieced together over the course of sixty years, with countless remodels turning it into a shopping maze. Several of the stores had open archways cut into their walls to allow customers free passage between them. There were communal storage spaces with their own exits and access to the roof. If Eddie moved fast enough, there was a good chance he'd disappear in the confusion of twists and turns and get away.

Running into the shopping arcade, Nate passed frightened shoppers who were running out. Some of them yelled that there was a man with a gun, but that didn't help Nate narrow down Eddie's location. In the midst of panicking people, reflections off glass storefront windows and shop display mirrors created an even more disorienting landscape.

Rios paused and Nate caught up with her. Both of them looked around and turned in a full circle, but saw nothing. Eddie could be anywhere. A couple of uniformed deputies hurried in from the Stagecoach Road side of the arcade. They hadn't seen him, either. "We're getting the civilians out of the way as fast as we can," a sheriff's department sergeant reported as he jogged up. "We've got everybody moving toward the park across the street. Keep searching and be careful."

"Right," Rios said. "I'll get Bubba." When she returned with the K-9, he determinedly led her toward a vintage clothing shop and then to a trio of simple frame dressing stalls in the back of the store. He strained toward the narrow gap at the bottom of one door and barked.

All of the deputies raised their guns.

Nate's lungs tightened. Bullets could start flying any minute and Lily was right there. What if she got hit?

"Come out or I'll sic my dog on you!" Rios called out. "He *will* bite you!"

Nate heard Lily plead, "Please, let me go."

"It's over," Eddie screamed. "You're too late! I'm not going to prison."

Rios flashed Nate a worried glance.

Terrified that Eddie was about to start shooting, Nate yanked open the door to the dressing stall next to the one Lily and Eddie were in. The sides to the stalls didn't reach the ceiling. Nate jumped, grabbed a narrow crossbeam and pulled himself up until he was crouched on top of it and looking down at Eddie and Lily.

Eddie was surrounded by the sound of his own

screaming and Bubba's barking, and he didn't realize Nate had climbed up there.

Nate could see that Eddie's shirt was completely sweat-soaked. It looked like he was crying. He still kept a tight grip on Lily, clutching her close to his body.

At least now Eddie held his gun pointed toward the ground. Maybe exhaustion was setting in. There might still be a chance he'd surrender.

But then Rios yelled out a final warning that she was about to release her dog.

"Do it!" Eddie screamed in response. He pointed his gun at Lily's head. His hand began to tighten around the handle and the trigger.

Nate saw it all. The quarters were too tight. Lily was too close to Nate's line of fire. It was the worst possible situation for him to try to shoot someone. But he had no choice. Nate took the shot.

Eddie dropped his gun and fell face-forward to the ground, crying out and gripping his shoulder where Nate had hit him. Lily screamed and dropped to the floor, covering her ears and desperately jamming herself into a back corner of the dressing stall.

Nate dropped down to the ground beside her just as Rios kicked open the door.

"Lily!"

She didn't respond to Nate. With her arms now wrapped tightly across her midsection, she seemed to be staring at something on the ground Nate couldn't see. He kneeled down and then sat on the floor beside her while Rios cuffed Eddie. Finally, Lily seemed to notice he was there and turned toward him.

"You okay?" he asked.

She straightened her glasses with trembling hands and shook her head.

"We have to get out of the way," Nate said gently.

EMTs were already trying to get to Eddie, who was cussing and wailing.

Nate stood, held out his hand and helped Lily to her feet. Then he held her close, trying to block her view of Eddie as they stepped out of the dressing stall and into the store.

As soon as they were out of the way Nate wrapped his arms around Lily and held her tight. He could feel her trembling, could feel her tears as they rolled from her face and onto his neck. But she still hadn't said anything.

The realization struck him that the story he told himself about not being family-man material was a lie. The truth was that he was just scared. Scared of failing someone who depended on him. Scared of losing someone he loved. Scared of loving and losing Lily.

He dropped his chin to the top of her head and let out a sigh. He was so very sorry she had to go through all this. And it still wasn't over. The cargo-theft ring was an extensive criminal enterprise. Eddie was only one piece of the puzzle.

Lily let herself melt into Nate's strong embrace. He had stayed with her from the moment this nightmare had started. She trusted him, and trusted he could chase away the dark imaginings that had formed in her mind after she'd heard the gunshot and seen the explosion of blood across Eddie Drake's shoulder.

For the moment she also felt comfort in the peace that traveled alongside her faith. *Thank You, Lord.*

"Nate!"

Someone called out for the deputy and he slowly, reluctantly, unwrapped his muscular arms from around Lily. She was feeling pretty reluctant about ending their embrace, too. But he had a job to do. And thanks to him she was already feeling a little bit stronger.

Sheriff Wolfsinger arrived on-scene a short time later. Nate was suspended, pending a full investigation, as was routine with the Oso County sheriff's department when one of their deputies was involved in a shooting.

"I don't think the investigation will take long," Sheriff Wolfsinger said. "But we're doing everything by the book."

Lily couldn't help thinking of Nate's enemies back in Copper Mesa. Everybody who was tied to the criminal element in the county and trying to undermine Nate's career would be having a field day. Old accusations, no matter how unfounded, would be dredged up and repeated in the news headlines until people started to believe them. It was just the way things worked these days.

While Nate and the sheriff talked, Nate stood close to Lily. He didn't exactly hold her hand, but he touched it a couple of times. Quietly. Unobtrusively. And Lily felt his concern for her wrap her from head to toe like a warm embrace. It didn't matter that he was back to wearing that tough-cop face. She now knew what lay behind it.

There might be some aspects to Nate Bedford's personality that he liked to hide, but he couldn't hide them from her anymore. If he didn't want to be a family man, that was one thing. But if he truly believed he didn't have what it took, he was mistaken. And Lily would have to set him straight.

Nate had more questions to answer and more people to talk to. Lily realized she was in the way and, after giving him a reassuring smile, she drifted toward a small table, where the dress shop's manager had set up a pot of coffee. She gave her statement to a deputy while sipping a cup, invigorated by the caffeine. Afterward, she reached into her pocket for her phone.

Oh yeah, her phone and purse were back at Nate's apartment, where she'd dropped them when Eddie grabbed her. It would be a short trip there and back. Eddie was in custody now. There were still cops in the shopping arcade. She'd make it quick.

A flurry of snowflakes tickled her face as she walked along the street outside the arcade. Most of the patrol cars that had lined the street earlier were gone now. Eddie had been hauled away in an ambulance. A forensics team was in the arcade documenting the physical evidence of the chase and shooting.

She walked the short distance to Nate's apartment, found her purse on the ground where she'd dropped it when Eddie grabbed her, picked it up and headed back. While she was walking, she dug her phone out of her purse. She'd better call her mom and let her know she was okay before she heard about what had just happened on the news.

The wind was picking up and Lily's cute jacket wasn't enough to keep her warm. Up ahead she saw Elijah's truck where Nate had left it by the park. There was probably something she could wrap around her shoulders in there.

There weren't many people on this secondary street

now. Everybody was already back to visiting the shops and restaurants around the arcade and over on Stage-coach Road.

She got to the truck, reached for the door handle and felt someone trying to get by on the sidewalk behind her. She moved forward a little to get out of the way, heard a whoosh and everything went black...

The next thing Lily knew she had a horrible head-ache. The back of her head not only hurt on the inside, but it also felt like her skull was actually sore. But wait, when and where had she fallen asleep?

Some kind of cloth lay atop her. Must be blankets pulled up over her head. She was probably in bed. Her thoughts still groggy, she reached up to move the blanket. It wasn't a blanket. It felt like a couple of coats had been thrown over her. She opened her eyes. They weren't her coats.

A jolt of fear cleared the grogginess and she sat up. A wave of dizziness washed over her. Her vision was fuzzy as she felt around for her glasses. Even with her bad eyesight, she could see that she was in the backseat of a car. And she could feel the car moving.

"What's happening?" The words felt heavy on her lips. She didn't get an answer, so she repeated her ques-tion more loudly. She could see that a man was driving the car and that the two of them were the only passen-gers.

Still feeling around the seat for her glasses, she tried to think. What did she last remember? Nate. She re-membered Nate. But that wasn't Nate driving the car. She could tell that much by the man's haircut. A sick feeling churned in her stomach. Something was terribly wrong. She tried to see the man's reflection in the rear-view mirror but her vision was just too blurry.

Fighting another wave of dizziness, she moved her body so she was facing forward and dropped her feet to the floor.

"You're awake," the driver said.

His voice was maddeningly familiar and held a hint of humor that felt disturbingly out of place.

"Who are you?" Lily asked, her voice still weak. "Where are we?"

"I'm your driver," the man answered breezily. "And we're going for a ride."

She knew that voice. Gripping the seat in front of her, she pulled herself forward to get a look at him. *"Bryan Torrent?"* The owner of Torrent Trucking? But that didn't make any sense.

"Sit back," he snapped. Then he lifted up a handgun from the seat beside him. Even without her glasses, Lily knew what it was.

Numb with fear, she sat back. *Dear Lord, what do I do now?*

FOURTEEN

Nate felt uncomfortable without his department-issued handgun, but surrendering it was part of the shooting after-incident procedure. He'd given his statement, filled out numerous forms—both electronic and paper—and watched as deputies from the next county arrived to take a look at the scene.

Having an outside agency step in and participate in the investigation of an officer-involved shooting was common. It helped avoid the accusation of a departmental cover-up. Nate was determined to do everything he could to help. A clean investigation would bolster the prosecution. And it might help diminish those old unfounded accusations that Nate operated outside the law.

A crime-scene photographer handed Nate a cup of coffee as he walked by and Nate took a sip. He glanced around the store, where the owner had just been given permission to start putting her disheveled shop back together. He blew out a breath and felt his neck muscles relax a little. That oily red-headed weasel Eddie Drake would be locked up as soon as his shoulder was stitched back together. He wouldn't be threatening Lily again.

"All right, Nate, *now* will you take a break? And by

that I mean head back to the Blue Spruce for a couple of days. I'm not going to be able to put you back on patrol until then, anyway."

Nate turned toward Sheriff Wolfsinger.

"I was just talking to our new county public information officer," the sheriff continued, gesturing with his phone. "Bit of a high-strung young man, anxious for a press release. I gave him the bare minimum information. I'm not hiding the fact that you were involved in the shooting, though. There's no reason to. You did a fine job."

Nate nodded. Sheriff Wolfsinger's praise was neither common nor elaborate, but it always felt sincere.

"I want to keep a lid on the rest of the story for now. The connection to Lily's hostage situation at the Starlight Mart. The fact that Drake was an employee at Torrent Trucking. Those facts don't need to be in the press release. Not with the cargo-theft investigation still ongoing."

Nate wanted to believe the part involving Lily was over. Surely an organized criminal ring with a reach spanning several states had much bigger concerns than whether or not an innocent woman had accidently overheard some small-fry drivers talking about an upcoming heist. Drivers who were going to be out of the loop and in prison for a long time. Whatever they thought Lily might have overheard must be old, useless information by now.

But the truth was organized crime groups did not maintain their power by letting troublesome people just walk away. Everyone would need to stay vigilant.

Sheriff Wolfsinger's phone rang. He put it up to his ear and walked away.

It looked as if Nate was officially off duty. He walked out of the store into the arcade, where a chilly wind blew through the passage. The small restaurants were bustling and the scent of beef sizzling over a mesquite fire made Nate's stomach growl.

Lily had to be hungry by now, too. Maybe they could have dinner together like normal people. Like a date.

He thought about their conversation in the truck riding into Painted Rock and inwardly cringed. She wasn't wrong, she'd just been hitting too close to home. And maybe he was a little bit envious. After everything she'd been through, from her problems with that idiot boyfriend at college to multiple attempts on her life, she'd found the courage to decide she was going to move forward with her life. Take new chances. Dare to hope.

Nate wanted the courage to do that, too. To dare to hope for a family of his own. Not just someday, but now. And to focus on the likelihood that he would make it through his work days just fine and wouldn't leave a family without their husband and father.

He walked around the arcade looking for Lily and those signature dark-framed glasses, but didn't see her. He walked through to Stagecoach Road and went up and down the street for a couple of blocks in each direction. No Lily.

An inner alarm sprang to life in the center of his chest, making his heart speed up, and he tried to quell it. She was around here somewhere. She was fine. He walked back through the arcade to the street that ran by the park and his apartment building. He'd spent quite a while dealing with the aftermath of the shooting, maybe Lily had called someone to come and take her home.

Maybe she'd had enough of him. He had acted like

a jerk when she'd tried to talk about a possible future together. He wouldn't blame her if she was angry with him.

He saw Rios by her patrol car, just standing there and watching the people on the street. There was a light scattering of snow on the ground, but snow wasn't falling right now. He walked up to the deputy. "Have you seen Lily?"

She turned to him and shook her head. "I haven't seen her in a while."

Nate's heart started to race again.

Rios spoke into her collar mic, asking if anyone had seen Lily. When no one responded, she began to ask specific deputies who'd been on-scene. No one had seen her recently. Nate glanced at the back of her patrol car. "Can you have Bubba look for her?"

"Sure." She turned to open the door of her patrol car and prepare her K-9 to get to work.

Nate headed back into the shopping arcade, found Wolfsinger and told him about his concern for Lily. The sheriff contacted dispatch to put out a call for everyone to be on the lookout for her.

Hoping he was worrying over nothing, Nate started walking, then running, back to his apartment. Maybe she was there. When he got to the truck he'd left parked on the side street, his heart fell to his feet. There on the ground, partially hidden by a snow-dusted juniper bush, were Lily's phone and purse. He picked them up. The purse had been knocked out of her hand outside his apartment when Eddie attacked her. Had she gone to retrieve it and someone grabbed her on the way back?

Nate once again ran into the shopping arcade, where he found the sheriff talking to Deputy Cooper. He showed them the purse and phone, told them where he'd found them and what he feared had happened.

Sheriff Wolfsinger got on his radio and ordered more resources up from Copper Mesa. He had Dispatch send out an emergency search bulletin for Lily with a digital image from her driver's license.

Then, turning toward Deputy Cooper, Wolfsinger gestured at a sheriff's department laptop that sat open on a table. "I know we collected exterior security video for the prosecutor's office to review later when they're putting together their case against Drake. Let's take a look at it now. See if we can find Lily on there."

Nate stood behind Cooper, impatiently watching over the deputy's shoulder as he opened up the video files and fast-forwarded through them. There were images of Eddie when he was in the car and holding Lily at gunpoint, but there was nothing showing a woman being abducted in the time frame after Eddie's capture and arrest. Cooper updated the video so they had everything from right after Eddie's capture to just a few minutes ago. They watched it several times but saw nothing that could help them.

Much as Nate wanted to race out to the truck and start searching for Lily right this minute, he forced himself to watch the video again and pay close attention. There *must* be some kind of clue. If it turned out she was somewhere in plain sight walking around town, the cops already out patrolling would find her. But what if she'd been grabbed and taken to some hidden place in the vast wildlands around Painted Rock? Nate might never find her.

No. It would do him no good to think like that.

Please, Lord, he prayed under his breath, *we need Your help*.

A few minutes later, Cooper opened a file that showed footage captured by a camera with a different angle. This time Nate saw what he needed.

On the video his beautiful Lily walked down the street toward the truck. Behind the truck was a large, gold luxury sedan. It was a make and model not commonly seen around Painted Rock. But Nate had seen a car like that recently.

When Lily stopped by the truck someone crept out of the bushes at the edge of the park, hat pulled down and coat collar flipped up to hide his face, and struck her on the back of the head.

Nate felt sick to his stomach as he watched the attack.

Lily slumped to the ground. The assailant hoisted her over his shoulder, carried her to the gold car and tossed her into the backseat. Then he got into the driver's seat and drove away.

Nate turned to Wolfsinger and the sheriff nodded. He recognized the car, too.

"Bryan Torrent," Nate growled, his fear for Lily quickly turning into anger and determination.

"Maybe," Wolfsinger said calmly. He contacted Dispatch to get the license plate number for Torrent's gold sedan. While he waited for a response he turned to Nate. "It might not be his car. If it is, someone might have stolen it." Nate nodded impatiently. His gut told him Torrent was involved, and Nate was itching to go get him.

"I know it's pointless for me to tell you not to go looking for Lily," the sheriff added. He turned to Deputy Cooper, asked him to get a handheld radio, then gave it to Nate when the deputy returned. "If you see something, let us know immediately."

Nate nodded his understanding as Dispatch got back to the sheriff with the license plate number and confirmation that the car belonged to Bryan Torrent, and that it had not been reported stolen.

A few minutes later Nate was back at the truck and hitting the speed-dial number for Elijah on his phone. Elijah picked up on the third ring.

"I need your tracking skills," Nate said as he started up the engine. "And I need help from Vanquish the Darkness." He quickly explained what had happened. "I need your members out on the roads and highways looking for the car."

"I'll head out now."

"No. I'm coming to pick you up. In your own truck, no less. I want you riding with me. I need your tracking expertise if they head out into the wildlands."

"I'll be ready and waiting."

"Make sure you're armed. We might not just be dealing with Torrent. We might be up against everyone involved with the cargo-theft operation."

"Like I said, brother. I'll be ready."

Sitting up in the backseat of the car, Lily pushed aside one of the coats Torrent had used to cover her when he'd knocked her unconscious and tried to hide her. Her fingertips brushed something oblong-shaped that felt like hard plastic. Her glasses. She quickly put them on. One of the lenses was cracked, but at least now she could see.

She looked out the window, hoping to get a sense of where they were. All she could see was darkness. They

were on a two-lane highway with other cars occasionally passing by. At least they weren't out in the middle
of nowhere. Not yet.

"Where are we going?"

"Oh, I think you know," Torrent answered, using
that oddly happy tone again. "But don't worry, it's not
too far out of town. Somebody will find your body by
next spring."

Trembling with a cold fear that went all the way
down to her bones, Lily looked up at the rearview mirror. Now that she had her glasses, she could see part of
Bryan Torrent's face.

He glanced into the mirror and their eyes met. "Yeah,
it's me. Go ahead and take a good look. Why not? Who
are you going to tell?"

So many questions swam through Lily's mind at once
that she had trouble focusing on a single one. Finally,
one thought pushed ahead of all the others. "Why?" The
cracked lens of her glasses made the headlights of the
cars passing by in the eastbound lane look distorted.
Her whole world felt upside down.

"Why am I here? Why are you doing this?" she demanded, her voice getting louder as anger shoved aside
her fear. Her boss had *kidnapped* her.

That was beyond crazy. It made no sense. "You *know*
I didn't overhear anything important," she said. "Some
random words. Stuff that *hinted* at criminal actions, but
none of it was specific. And none of it had anything to
do with *you*."

"Oh, you must have heard a little more than what
you're admitting to," Torrent answered. He met her
gaze in the rearview mirror again. "Your friends from
the sheriff's department showed up to watch my busi-

ness on what was supposed to be a pivotal night. How would they have known to do that unless you told them to? Good thing we changed our plans when that idiot Jack Covert got arrested trying to grab you in your own house."

"But you're in the clear," Lily said, trying to reason with him. "No one suspects you of anything. I don't understand why we're here now." Fear was starting to overpower her anger again and her voice shook. But she was also sick and tired of being chased and attacked.

"I don't even know why you're…" She'd started to say "why you're going to kill me," but quickly decided that was a bad idea. "I don't know why you're bringing me here," she said instead.

"Your life is going to end out here tonight because people believe you know things that really aren't your business."

"But I don't know anything," she said. "I did hear something about early Wednesday, but nothing specific. The deputies were there just in case something did happen."

"You know, you've stuck to that story and I believe you," Torrent said softly. "But the truth doesn't matter. Appearances matter. And it appears to my business associates that you know information that could cause them trouble. They think you know enough to tie me and my company to their very lucrative business endeavors. And that you might tell the cops all about it. They've made it clear to me that I have to make sure that doesn't happen. So you have to go."

Lily considered opening the door and jumping out, but they were moving at high speed and the chances she'd survive were slim. That would be her last resort.

She looked at the coats. Maybe she could open a window, wave a coat and get someone's attention as they passed by. She could scream and wave and hope they called the cops.

"You're getting quiet back there," Torrent said. "I hope you're not up to anything."

Lily saw headlights. A car headed toward them from the opposite direction. She grabbed a coat and hit a button to roll down the window. Nothing happened. The window didn't move. Torrent started to laugh.

She pulled the door handle, figuring she'd throw the coat in front of the oncoming car. The door wouldn't open.

"Childproof locks," Torrent said in a singsong voice. "Can't be too careful."

Lily snapped. She reached over Torrent's shoulder to grab the steering wheel and managed to jerk it to the right a little before he shoved her aside. It was enough to make the car leave the highway and drive into the sandy soil. Torrent hit the brakes, tossing up a shower of sand and rocks behind the car.

Lily flew back into the seat, but while the car was still moving she got up again. She lurched forward over the front seat, reaching for the keys and trying to turn off the engine.

The car suddenly stopped and Lily fell forward, the top half of her body landing in the front seat. Before she could right herself, Torrent grabbed her by the neck. Then he seized one of her hands and pulled the rest of her body down into the front seat.

Lily screamed and twisted, but she couldn't break free of his grasp. He let go of her hand long enough to open his door. Then he got out, pulling Lily out with him.

She prayed that someone in a passing car was paying attention. That they could somehow see what was happening out here even though it was dark and they'd call for help.

Torrent spun her around, yanking her hands behind her back and tying her wrists together with what felt like a leather belt. Fueled by terror, Lily jerked free and started to run. He easily caught her and dragged her back to his car. She struggled and screamed as loudly as she could as he shoved her into the backseat.

Nate stopped where the Morales ranch driveway met the highway and waited with the truck engine idling.

Elijah was already there, sitting in his wife's sedan since Nate was driving Elijah's truck. Olivia was next to her husband, a phone held up to her ear. Jonathan sat in the backseat.

Elijah gave his wife a kiss and got out of the car carrying a rifle and night-vision goggles. Jonathan climbed out of the backseat, then reached back in to grab a black backpack and a coil of lightweight climbing rope.

The members of Vanquish the Darkness were good friends to have when you were in trouble.

"I appreciate your help," Nate said as the men got into the truck. "I know this is your rig—" he turned to Elijah "—but I'm driving."

"I understand."

"I'm sorry about what happened to Lily," Jonathan said from the backseat. "But we'll find her. We won't give up. Ever."

Nate turned to face him. "I appreciate that."

"Olivia's been on the phone since you called us," Elijah said. "We've already got over a dozen people out looking for Lily. More will join in as they hear about it."

"Thank you." This wasn't the first time Nate had been grateful for assistance from the Christian biker group. But this whole situation with Lily was the first time their help had felt so personal to him.

The police radio propped on the seat beside him crackled with sporadic conversation. Every time a transmission started, Nate hoped it would be a lead on Lily. So far it hadn't been. Just routine deputy business.

"You're a tracker," Nate said to Elijah. "How do we start tracking Lily?"

"I hate to say this," Elijah answered in a somber voice, "but whoever grabbed her probably means to kill her and dump her body where she won't be found."

For a few seconds Nate couldn't breathe. Of course, he'd already thought of that, but hearing it said out loud made it seem much more possible.

"God is still God," Jonathan said from the backseat. "Hang on to that."

"Amen," Elijah said quietly.

Please, Lord, Nate prayed simply, trusting that God knew all that was in his heart.

"If I wanted to kill someone, dispose of them and get away unseen I'd do it northwest of town," Elijah said.

Nate was glad Elijah fought on the side of good.

"There are fewer ranch houses out there," Elijah continued. "Plus there's forest for cover and canyons where you can hide. I think we should head in that direction."

Nate breathed out another prayer as he hit the accelerator and took the necessary turns to get him out of town. Once he was clear of Painted Rock, he shot down the highway and hoped one of his coworkers didn't try to pull him over for speeding.

FIFTEEN

Torrent turned off the highway shortly after he tied Lily's wrists together and tossed her into the backseat of his car.

Lily looked out the window to get some sense of where they were. But as they drove down the rutted dirt road he'd turned onto, all she could see was the darkness beside her and a few stray snowflakes sliding across the beam of the headlights in front.

Torrent finally stopped, got out, came around and pulled her out of the car. She stumbled and fell.

Lily braced herself. Would there be a quick, single shot? She struggled to get to her feet, trying to pull her wrists free of their binding, but she lost her balance and fell back down. Cold, watery snowflakes swirled downward from the scattering clouds and melted on her face. The coolness revived her a little and once again outrage nudged aside fear. He hadn't immediately shot her. She still had a chance.

Torrent reached down to grab her upper arm and pull her to her feet. She lay there like deadweight. Why make it easy for him?

"Get up," he snapped. This time he used both hands

to pick her up. Then he pulled his gun out of the waist-band of his pants, pointed it at her, spun her around and shoved her toward a rocky, dry creek bed that led into the mouth of a small, narrow canyon. She resisted. This looked like the end of the line. If she went into that canyon she'd never come out alive.

"It's not too late to let me go," she said, trying to stall for time. "I'm nobody. No one would take my word against yours. They'd never believe we were ever out here if you deny it."

"Walk." He shoved her into the mouth of the canyon.

"Where are we?" Lily looked up at the rim of the canyon rising a hundred feet above her head.

An insistent breeze made her shiver, while overhead the clouds were breaking apart and moving on. Filtered moonlight shone down, but it was still hard to see where she was walking on the rocky ground. It was even harder keeping her balance with her hands tied behind her back.

Torrent ignored her question and pushed her to stay near the canyon wall. The ground rose in elevation the farther back they went. He must be taking her to the very back to kill her. If she was smart, she'd just stop walking and get it over with.

Apparently she was more stubborn than smart. She kept walking while trying to think of a way she could escape.

She tugged at the leather binding her wrists. Maybe she could loosen it if she kept working it.

"Where are we going?" she asked again, surprised at how normal her voice sounded.

Torrent didn't answer, but after a few more steps they stood in front of a tumbledown single-room wooden

shack built on a slight ledge. It was barely visible for
the trees and bushes that had grown up around it. "We
aren't going anywhere anymore," Torrent answered in
a silky tone. "We're here."

Torrent was quiet for a moment, then he looked down
and shook his head. When he looked up, he wore a sad
smile.

Lily thought of her mom and tears sprang to her eyes.
And then she thought of Nate. At least he wasn't here
with her, which meant he was okay. He was safe. He
was probably worried about her, but he would survive.
Even if she didn't.

Lily tried to swallow but her throat was dry. She continued to stare at Torrent, waiting for the flash at the
end of the gun barrel.

"My inheritance is gone," Torrent said softly.

"What?" Maybe something inside him was so dark
and twisted that nothing he could say would ever make
sense, but engaging in conversation might buy Lily
some time. "What happened?" she asked.

He'd brought her to the exposed lip of rock in front
of the tumbledown shack. He took the step up, let go
of her and turned to face her, as though he was standing on a stage. He seemed to like to talk about himself.
Maybe she could use that against him.

Torrent tilted his head to the side and gave her an
appraising look. She stopped tugging at the binding on
her wrists while he was watching her so closely.

As soon as he was distracted she would start trying
to get loose again.

"I inherited some small businesses from my parents,"
he said. "One by one, they began to fail, so I cashed
out and sold them. I don't like things that are slow and

tedious. I like things that are exciting. I like to gamble. The money from the businesses fueled my gambling and I did well for a while."

He glanced away and Lily pulled hard on the belt on her wrists a couple of times.

"Then my wife got sick," Torrent continued. He turned back to Lily. Now his expression was an angry, piercing stare. "We knew early on that recovery was a long shot. But I'd won a few long shots so I thought there might be a chance. The treatments didn't work. My wife was in pain. I needed more money to take care of her, plus a few extra bucks to help lift my spirits. So I took a gambling trip to Vegas. And I lost. A lot. Afterward, I got a visit in my hotel room. A man offered me a line of credit to earn back what I'd lost. Of course, I'd have to pay a small fee. I took the loan, sure I could win it back. I didn't. Torrent Trucking was the collateral."

His shoulders slumped and he took a deep breath.

"My wife died," Torrent said flatly. "Everyone believes the insurance money was enough to help me recover financially. The truth is, I get a monthly payment for letting some people out of Vegas use my company. We make it look as if I'm still running it. They're probably involved in the cargo thefts, but I don't ask questions."

"So the two men who tried to kill me were working for you?"

"No." Torrent shook his head. "Several of my employees were fired. New employees like you were hired because they wouldn't notice any changes. Those two drivers who tried to kill you were hired by the people who are now running my company. They talked when they should not have and you overheard them. They tried to kill you because they were terrified of what would happen to them if their bosses heard about it.

"Eddie was brought in by the Vegas people for his computer and hacking expertise. He, too, was terrified some bit of information you'd overheard would get him killed by the company's new owners. That's why he tried to shoot you on the highway.

"If the whole operation gets busted, I lose my income. So I did what I could to keep Eddie scared and I was there to watch him grab you tonight. My plan was for him to die in a hail of police gunfire. That obviously didn't work. But then I couldn't believe my good fortune when you walked outside of that shopping arcade and right to me."

"Did Eddie Drake kill Sheila?"

"She was enamored with Eddie. And you know how much he likes to blabber about himself to impress the ladies." Torrent sighed. "If he hadn't already told her too much, he would have eventually. So I took care of it. I told him the new owners were in town and they'd killed Sheila. And that he'd be next if he didn't get to you tonight."

"*Are* the people who own your business in town?"

"They're staying away, but they're watching. And if they aren't happy, I'm in big trouble."

He sighed heavily but didn't say anything else. His story was at an end. The binds on Lily's hands weren't free, but they were looser. If she was going to do something, she needed to do it now.

She took off to her right, running as fast as she could. There were some thick trees to the side of the canyon, and big boulders farther in. She only needed a place to hide and a minute to work her hands free. Then she could move faster. She'd be able to climb. She could get away.

Torrent cursed and called out her name. She made a couple of turns and heard him chasing after her, but then she heard him going in the wrong direction, away from her.

She crouched down behind a large boulder. There was a small pine tree behind her and she managed to slide a slender branch beneath the leather binding and get her hands free.

She could now see the leather belt he'd used to tie her wrists. After shaking it off and letting it fall to the ground, she brought her hands in front of her and rubbed her wrists.

If she stayed in the small canyon, Torrent was sure to find her. She had to make her way back to the canyon entrance and out into the wilderness, where she at least had a chance of hiding in the darkness. She took a deep breath to fortify herself, then crouched down low and moved around the boulder.

Torrent stood in her way.

"Change of plans," he said dryly. He grabbed her by the hair and pulled her close to him. Then he started walking, shoving a gun into her ribs and forcing her to keep up with him. "Forget the cabin. I was going to be nice, shoot you in there and make it quick. But I'm not feeling so nice anymore."

Lily stumbled, her knees weak with fear, and he yanked her back to her feet.

"There's a lovely little waterfall at the back of the canyon with a small pool at the bottom. It hasn't frozen over yet. Beautiful spot. Families have been coming out here to splash around in the summer for generations."

"Let go of me," Lily shrieked in a panic, fighting to pull away from him.

He dropped her hair and clamped his hand around her arm, holding her tighter. "*No!* I already lost everything once. Thanks to you, I could lose it all again. You're going into the pond. I might fire a shot or two into you to speed things up, but I *am* going to watch you shiver until you sink down into the water and stay there." He looked at her with strangely empty eyes and grinned. "Just think how pretty you'll look when true winter sets in and the water freezes solid."

Nate drove west on the county highway north of Painted Rock, watching the light snow falling in the dark night and thinking about Lily and how important she'd become to him in such a short amount of time. She accepted people just as they were. She seemed to have trouble forgiving herself for some of the decisions she'd made, but Nate saw her work through that and it had helped him get better at accepting himself and the rough childhood he'd survived.

He could see himself with a family of his own now. And he'd started imagining Lily in his future. The truth was he didn't want to imagine a future without her.

He pushed aside the dark thoughts gathering in his mind and cleared his throat. "Did you have a particular destination in mind where we should look out here?" he asked Elijah. He hadn't had much time to patrol in the wilderness since he'd been assigned to Painted Rock. He stayed busy with calls closer to town.

"There's another county road that intersects with this one about twenty miles ahead of us."

"Yeah. There's a gas station and a truck stop there."

"Right," Elijah confirmed. "It's worth stopping there to see if anybody's seen anything that could help us. Maybe Torrent had to stop for gas. If he's taking Lily much farther out into the wilderness he's got to fuel up somewhere."

"All right." Nate wanted to find Lily *right now*. Talking to people along the highway felt like a feeble way to track down and rescue the woman he loved. But at the moment it was all he had.

There wasn't much conversation about Lily on the police radio. But since anybody could easily listen in on that, the sheriff's department often used cell phones to share important information. Nate pulled his phone from his pocket and handed it to Elijah, asking him to connect it to the hands-free system. "Let's call Rios."

Before Elijah could place the call to her, a radio transmission came through. A citizen had called in to report witnessing some kind of altercation between a man and woman beside the highway. The general location given was on the highway Nate was now traveling, heading in the same direction and just a few miles ahead. Elijah's instincts had been right.

A deputy responded from the truck stop Nate and Elijah had just been talking about, confirming that he'd heard the transmission and that he'd start looking for the man and woman in question.

At the end of the transmission Elijah put through the call to Rios. The only detail she could add was that the vehicle was described as a large light-colored car. Certain they were on the right track, Nate drove even faster.

Elijah called his wife so she could update the members of Vanquish the Darkness. After he ended his call, Jonathan spoke up from the backseat. "What if Torrent didn't go all the way to the truck stop? What if he turned off onto some road in the wilderness before then?"

Nate glanced at Elijah, hoping for a helpful response.

"I can only think of one road he could drive very far on in a sedan," Elijah said after thinking for a minute. "Most of the roads around here are just cleared paths for off-roaders. But he could drive his car out to Heart Canyon. The canyon is fairly shallow and an easy climb. There's a waterfall in spring. People take kids out there. The county keeps the road graded so cars can make it through."

"Then that's where we're going."

"It's about seven or eight miles ahead."

Nate's focus stayed riveted on Lily as he drove, his thoughts bouncing back and forth between fear that she was in grave danger, and hope that they would both make it through this night and have a life together. Maybe he didn't know from experience what a normal family was like, but he knew what *his* family was like. Bud, Ellen and his adoptive brother, Gaston. They were a family. What Nate didn't know about being a husband and father, he was determined to figure out. Fear had held him back from being a family man, but it wouldn't any longer. He'd trusted God with so many things. He could trust Him to help Nate with raising a healthy family. If Lily would have him. If she loved him as he loved her.

"Slow down, we're almost there," Elijah called out.

A few seconds later Nate made the turn onto a snow-dusted road.

"There aren't any tracks in the snow," Nate said, his heart sinking like lead. "Torrent must not have turned down here."

"It only stopped snowing a few minutes ago," Jonathan said. "Snow could have fallen on their tracks and covered them. Don't lose hope, man."

The road curved. As Nate drove around a bend, his headlights splashed across an object that looked like an oblong boulder.

Driving closer, he saw Bryan Torrent's car, easily identifiable despite the speckling of snow on it.

Nate's blood felt like fire and ice shooting through his veins. He would rescue Lily and stop Torrent. Didn't matter what he had to do. "Call Sheriff Wolfsinger." He ground out the words at Jonathan. "Tell him where we are."

Nate slammed on the brakes, killed the truck's engine and threw open his door. He got out and hurried toward the car, scanning the ground for tracks. Elijah stepped in front of him. Nate stepped to the side and Elijah got in front of him again.

"We're going to be smart about this," Elijah said.

Nate impatiently stepped around him a second time, but as he did a quiet inner voice told him Elijah was right. Staying calm in a horrible situation saved lives. He couldn't let his feelings for Lily cloud his good judgment. Not when she needed him most. He paused and nodded at Elijah.

Elijah reached into the truck for his rifle and the coil of climbing rope. He grabbed the backpack from beside his brother in the backseat, took out a handgun and passed it to Nate. "It's loaded."

Nate took a couple seconds to check out the gun and then tucked it into the waistband of his jeans.

"That's the entrance to the canyon." Elijah gestured toward a large fissure in the wall of rock across from them.

It just took a few seconds to spot partial footprints in the shallow, sparse snow. Nate quickly followed them for a few feet until he was certain they were leading to the mouth of the canyon.

Jonathan got out of the truck and caught up with Nate and Elijah. "Cavalry's on the way."

"I'm not waiting," Nate said. "You two stay here and make sure no one goes into the canyon behind me. Could be a trap. And it'll speed things up if you can wave the deputies over when they arrive."

"Got it," Jonathan said.

"You're not doing this alone," Elijah warned. "Give me time to get up to the rim of the canyon. It doesn't go back very far and I can climb down to the floor at the other end. It's not a far drop to the bottom. We can box in Torrent and Lily and whoever else might be in there."

A good plan, but Nate wasn't waiting any longer.

"Move fast," Nate said as he stepped around Elijah and walked into the canyon.

Nate stayed close to the wall, moving as carefully and quietly as possible. He stopped to listen several times, but the only noise he heard was the faint wind-blown sound of cars passing by on the highway in the distance.

He looked at the ground for tracks, but couldn't see anything obvious. Didn't matter—he was pretty sure Torrent had taken Lily into the farthest depth of the canyon to make certain there were no witnesses.

He reached the old shack Elijah had mentioned and paused outside, watching and listening. Nothing. Slowly, he stepped up onto the slab of rock that served as a front porch and then through the door, bracing himself to see Lily's lifeless body.

The shack was empty. She wasn't there. Relief washed over him. But then terror gripped his heart. What if Torrent had simply swapped out vehicles here? What if he'd gotten back on the highway in a different car? What if Nate never found Lily?

As he stood there disheartened, he heard a sound at the end of the canyon. He hurried in that direction, hearing more sounds as he drew closer to the source. The noises seemed to be coming from ground level, but also from up on the rim. Had Elijah had enough time to get up there or was someone else watching him?

Nate shoved past trees and spiky bushes and into the clearing at the base of a trickling waterfall at the end of the canyon. He saw an odd shape there, and at first he couldn't understand what he was looking at. Then he knew. It was Lily, lying on a large flat rock beside the small pool at the bottom of the waterfall.

She was still and unmoving. He was too late.

No!

Nate rushed toward her. At the same time he sensed movement up on the canyon rim. If someone was up there watching him, if this was a trap, he didn't care. Lily might still be alive! And if she stayed out here any longer she would freeze to death. Her jacket and shoes were gone. She had only jeans and a T-shirt to protect her from the bone-chilling temperatures.

Nate dropped to his knees beside her and touched her skin. She was alive! Weak, but alive. She tried to speak but she was shaking and her teeth were chattering so badly he couldn't understand her.

Nate tore off his coat, gently lifted her to a sitting position and wrapped the coat around her trembling shoulders. "Are you wounded?" he asked, terrified that she was already too far gone. "Have you been shot?"

She shook her head. And then he saw the large bruise that covered half of her face. Her broken glasses were on the ground a few feet away.

He pulled off his cowboy hat and tried to put it on her, but she wouldn't stop shaking her head.

"Bryan Torrent. He's here," she finally said clearly enough for him to understand, her voice a weak whisper.

"I haven't seen him," Nate said, kneeling down and holding her close to his body.

"I'm right here."

Nate whirled toward the voice and something smacked him in the face. It hit hard enough to knock him backward and wrench Lily from his arms.

Momentarily stunned, Nate couldn't see anything, couldn't even get his eyes open. His head was spinning and he couldn't regain his balance. Finally he managed to get himself onto his hands and knees. He crawled around on the sandy ground, desperately trying to find his way back to Lily.

Torrent laughed, stomped on Nate's hand and grabbed the handgun from Nate's waistband.

Then he kicked him in the stomach, knocking the wind out of him and rolling him onto his back. Nate finally got his stinging eyelids to open. The first thing he saw was Lily. He fought to stand and steady his feet beneath him so he could get to her.

He wasn't fast enough. Torrent grabbed Lily and started yanking her to her feet.

But then Nate saw something by the waterfall behind Lily and Torrent. It was moving down the side of the canyon wall, from one rocky shelf to the next. Nate tried to focus his eyes, not certain if it was a falling rock or a shadow.

It took him a moment to see in a beam of moonlight that it was Elijah.

Torrent appeared to see Elijah at the same time and he hesitated. Those few seconds gave Nate the time he needed to take a few shaky strides and throw a punch that knocked Torrent to the ground.

Seconds later, Elijah was there making sure Torrent wouldn't escape.

Nate turned to Lily, wrapped his arms around her and held on tight. If he had his way, he would never, ever, let her go.

SIXTEEN

Lily was wearing two coats. She had on Nate's, plus a raincoat he'd borrowed from a responding deputy. He'd also fetched a blanket from the EMTs and draped it over her shoulders. But it was having Nate holding her close with his arms wrapped around her that truly made her feel warm.

Snowflakes were falling again, but they were sparse and lazy. Jonathan had moved Elijah's truck to the mouth of the canyon and Nate and Lily were now leaning against it and watching the sheriff's department take care of business. Lily was finally dry and warm. Nate had been holding an ice pack up to his right cheek for a while, but at least nothing was broken. Lily had also been holding an ice pack up to her own cheek until just a few minutes ago.

Bryan Torrent had been treated for the punches he'd taken and was now seated in the back of an idling patrol car. Sheriff Wolfsinger was walking around in the canyon making sure that all the forensic documentation was being done correctly.

Once Lily had warmed up inside a patrol car she'd been reluctant to leave the crime scene. Turned out Nate felt the same way. They both wanted to see this thing wrapped up, see Bryan Torrent driven away in a patrol car and know it was all over. When Lily got out of the patrol car and she and Nate walked over to lean against Elijah's truck, Jonathan had thoughtfully made himself scarce. Elijah was off talking to a few members of Vanquish the Darkness, who'd showed up in case their help was needed.

Lily was also waiting around because she didn't want her time with Nate to come to an end. Even though their relationship had formed under the worst of circumstances, she had come to love being around Nate. She was used to seeing him every day. She wasn't ready to say goodbye and head back down to her mom's house in Copper Mesa alone.

During their last conversation driving into Painted Rock, she'd tried to tell Nate how she felt about him. About *them*. She'd fished around to see if he thought they might possibly have a future together. But he was still so uncertain about having a family life, so edgy when she tried to talk about it, that it started to seem like the best way she could show her appreciation for all he'd done would be to just leave him alone. She knew in her heart he would always look out for her and protect her. That he would drop everything and come to her rescue if she ever asked. Maybe she should be happy with that.

No, she wouldn't be happy with just that. And she wasn't going to let him off the hook that easily.

"So, you were just going to rush up into the canyon and rescue me single-handed?" she asked, nudging him with her elbow and then looking at him.

A charmingly self-conscious grin spread across his swollen face. "If I had to, yes."

He almost hadn't arrived in time. Torrent was just about to shoot Lily and push her in the water when he'd heard noises. Afraid his gunshots would give away his location to anyone who might be searching for Lily, he'd hit her and knocked her down instead, threatened to kill her if she made a sound or tried to get away. Then he'd hidden among the trees until Nate showed up.

"You're going to be bored when you go back to your normal life," she teased.

"I don't know." He reached up and touched his swollen cheek. "It's kind of nice to go through a day without getting smacked in the face with a tree branch."

"Yeah, but what about the rest of it? Aren't you going to miss that?"

The sound of a dog barking caught their attention and Deputy Rios walked up with Bubba. They'd been the first to arrive after Jonathan called in their location and they'd found Torrent's car.

"Glad to see you're both in good shape," she said as she smiled at them. "I've been wanting to get over here and chat with you for a while, but you know how it is. Got to take care of business."

"I understand," Nate said. "We've both given our statements a couple of times." Then he reached out and gave Rios a playful punch on the arm. "Thanks for showing up."

The deputy shrugged. "What if you'd gotten killed out here and your replacement was even more obnoxious than you are? I wouldn't want to get stuck working with someone like that."

Nate grinned. "Good thinking."

"Well, I'd love to stay and chat, but I'm still on duty," Rios said. "So I'll see ya."

Rios and Bubba sauntered away and Nate turned to Lily, reaching down to take each of her hands in his. "So, I think we were talking about getting back to normal life when we were interrupted."

Lily looked up at him. It was starting to snow a little harder, the flakes swirling and landing on the brim of his cowboy hat. Her heart began to melt at the touch of his hands and the warmth in his eyes.

"I've been an idiot," he said.

"No argument there," she joked.

Nate shook his head. "Please, can you let me finish?" He cleared his throat. "I've spent a lot of years keeping my distance from people. Figuring if I even tried to have a family I wouldn't know what to do and I'd just mess it up." He took a breath, started again. "Look, there's a lot I've figured out but I don't know how to say it. Normal life for me was to be on my own. To try and control as much as I could and when it came to my personal life, to play it safe. But I realize now I don't want normal anymore." He looked into her eyes. "I want you."

Lily grinned. "I don't want normal, either."

"I never meant to fall in love with you." He reached out to brush his fingertips across her forehead and tuck her disheveled hair behind her ear. "But I did. I love you, Lily Doyle."

Lily felt her grin slowly dissolve. She had fallen in love with him, too. But she hadn't realized how hard or how deeply she'd fallen until this very moment. "I love you, too."

Nate moved closer and leaned down toward her.

"Nate! Good work." Sheriff Wolfsinger strode up to

them. "Lily." He touched the brim of his cowboy hat and nodded.

Lily nodded back, trying to be friendly when she really wanted him to go away so she could get back to her conversation with Nate.

"Well, Bryan Torrent hasn't told us any details of the cargo-theft operation he told *you* about," he said, glancing at Lily. "But he might decide he wants to eventually. Now that we've got four of these lowlifes in custody we can start looking at their phone records, where they've traveled, what they've bought." He turned his attention to Nate. "This will give the task force a lot to work with. We'll break them down eventually."

"We will," Nate agreed, nodding.

Sheriff Wolfsinger looked back at Lily. "Now that this has blown open, I doubt we have to worry about you anymore. Whatever those guys were talking about the night you overheard them is obsolete information by now. I think the point of killing you was to make sure no one knew about Torrent's connection to what happened to you, about his connection to the ongoing cargo thefts across the state, or about the organized crime link to his trucking company. All of that will be the top news story across the region by morning. I'll make sure of it."

"That's a relief," Lily said. "Thank you."

Wolfsinger nodded and then his phone rang. He sighed and put it up to his ear as he turned and walked toward his patrol car.

Nate grabbed Lily around her waist and pulled her close for a kiss, his lips warm in the cool air and his touch strong and gentle. Lily sighed and felt her whole body relax against his. It felt like going home.

They heard the exaggerated sound of someone clearing his throat. This time it was Jonathan. "Hey, lovebirds, sorry to interrupt."

Nate glared at him.

Jonathan grinned back. "The weatherman says we've got a pretty good snowstorm headed this way so this might be a good time to pack up and head out."

"But you'll have to plan on staying in your old rooms at our ranch tonight," Elijah added as he walked up. "My mom insists. And you know she cooks when she's worried. Apparently there's enough food at the house to feed an army." He and Jonathan got into the front seats of his truck. Nate pulled open the door to the backseat. Lily climbed in and he got in after her.

Inside the truck, Nate reached for Lily's hand. After giving it a gentle squeeze, he lifted it up and brushed his lips across her knuckles. Then he brought her hand to his chest until it rested above his heart. "I'm never letting go of you," he said quietly, as Elijah started the truck's engine and Jonathan made a call on his phone.

Lily couldn't see Nate's face very well in the dim light, but she heard the vulnerability in his voice and felt tears begin to form in the corners of her eyes. She thought about everything he'd been through since he was a child, and how much courage it took for him to open his heart to her.

"Don't worry," she said softly, squeezing his hand just a little bit tighter. "I'm never letting go of you, either."

EPILOGUE

Six months later

"I can't stop thinking about that cake," Nate said. He stole a quick glance at the pink box on the bench seat of his truck and then turned to Lily. He smiled at her and she felt the surface of her skin warm. "Maybe we could just pull over and eat it," he said. "We could grab a replacement cake from the grocery store."

They'd spent the early afternoon at the wedding photographer's studio in Copper Mesa. As soon as they'd left the studio, Ellen had texted Nate and asked him to pick up a cake she'd ordered at a small bakery in town. It was a chocolate ganache–covered confection perfect for the barbecue dinner Ellen had planned for tonight. She'd insisted on giving them an engagement dinner and agreed to keep it small and intimate.

"If we'd taken my car, there'd be forks in the glove box and we could dig in right now," Lily said.

It was so good to spend time with Nate just driving around, doing simple, everyday things like running errands. With nobody trying to kill them.

In the last few months they'd both been working hard, Nate with law enforcement duties and Lily with her job at the catering company, which, surprisingly, had turned into a full-time job. She'd been able to pay off her debt and get a little money saved. There were several nice cafés in Painted Rock. Once she and Nate got married and she moved up there, she should be able to find a job fairly easily. Maybe even open her own place one day.

Nate made the turn onto the road to the Blue Spruce Ranch and then a short time later he reached the ranch entrance. Balloons and streamers were tied to the stone pillars. Nate's big orange cat sat beneath one of the balloons, looking up as if he was trying to figure out a way to grab the thing.

"Wow, Ellen really went all out for our dinner party," Lily said as Nate steered his truck up the drive.

Nate reached for her hand and squeezed it.

And then Lily's eye caught a glimpse of shiny metal. Farther up the drive, a row of motorcycles were parked with military precision. "Looks like some riders from Vanquish the Darkness are here," she said.

Nate gave her a puzzled look. "Yeah, I recognize Elijah's bike."

Smiling, Lily crossed her arms over her chest. "I think this is going to be something more than the small party Ellen promised." No wonder Ellen's friend, Belinda, had fiddled around for so long finishing up the cake they'd been sent to pick up. It had been an excuse to keep them away from the ranch.

"Well, two can play at that game." Nate pulled over onto a patch of dirt. "Let's park down here, sneak up and surprise *them*."

"Great idea."

They got out. Lily carried the cake. They tried to be stealthy, but they were quickly caught by two alert canine sentries.

"Hey, little mosquito dogs," Nate greeted Abby and Beatrice when they ran around the corner of the house and barreled straight toward them.

Lily glanced around. "Mom must be nearby."

Nate bent down to pet Beatrice. Abby stayed back, as usual. And then finally she came forward and let him pet her.

Nate picked up both dogs. They looked even tinier in his big hands. Both girls wagged their tails and were clearly happy to be held by Nate.

Lily knew the feeling.

"Guess this means you're finally, officially welcomed into the family," she said to Nate. His tough exterior might not have changed since the night they'd first crossed paths at the Starlight Mart, but these days he trusted her enough to let her see the sweeter emotions behind it.

They walked around the corner of the house. At first, no one saw them. Lily's gaze swept across the beautiful late-spring lawn, where lots of friends and family were gathered. Kids and dogs ran around. Steaks sizzled on a grill. Lily's mom stood chatting with Elijah and Olivia Morales. A little farther away, Crystal Rios and Gaston were walking out of the stables, Bubba trotting behind them.

And sitting at a beautifully decorated table with Bud and Ellen were Joseph Suh's parents and his sister, Joanna. The Suhs had no idea how much their compassion and the goodness of their son had worked to complete Lily's life. She would make a point of going over and telling them. Joseph Suh's kind heart was still bringing about good in the world even after he was gone.

"You know," Lily said, "over the last few months there were so many times I thought I was at a dead end.

Literally, when people were pointing guns at me and trying to kill me. But even before that, when I made stupid decisions and I couldn't see how there was a plan for my life. I was certain I'd messed everything up beyond repair. I'm so glad I was wrong." She turned to Nate, her eyes starting to tear up a little.

Nate just stared at her, still holding the dogs.

"Well," she finally demanded, starting to get annoyed, "what do you think?"

He glanced at the crowd, then at the pink box still in her hands, and raised his eyebrows. "I think we're going to need a bigger cake."

She rolled her eyes and made a scoffing sound, at which point he leaned down to kiss her. The dogs squirmed in his hands.

Somebody let out a loud whoop. It sounded like Bud. A whistle came from Gaston's direction. Leaning back from Nate's kiss, Lily felt her face burn. But she also felt herself smile.

The guests started applauding. Nate set down the dogs, reached for Lily's hand and squeezed it. "Guess it's time to face this unruly crowd together."

"Yep." Lily squeezed his hand in return and grinned. "Let me show you how it's done."

* * * * *

If you loved this story, don't miss Jenna Night's first heartstopping romance

LAST STAND RANCH

Find this and other great reads at www.LoveInspired.com

Dear Reader,

Looking ahead in life isn't always easy. Especially when there are things in your past that you wish you could fix or change.

Deputy Nate Bedford worried that his tragic and unstable childhood left him without the resources to be a good father. Yet those very experiences gave him the compassion and drive to help others. Lily Doyle made some unwise decisions and was tempted to believe her life was ruined beyond repair. But in the process of recovering from her mistakes, she was reminded that we don't have to be perfect people to be worthy of love.

With God's grace and the help of family and good friends, we find we can keep moving forward even when we think we can't. I hope when you face difficult times you'll press on in faith and keep on going one step at a time.

You can find me at my website, Jennanight.com. Or at my Jenna Night page on Facebook. I retweet my fair share of cute animal pictures on Twitter @Night_Jenna. Or if you feel so inclined, shoot me an email at Jenna@jennanight.com. I'd love to hear from you.

Jenna Night

LISCNM0617

Get 2 Free Books,

Plus 2 Free Gifts —

just for trying the Reader Service!

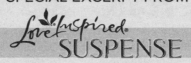
A simple twitch of his finger and his sister's killer would
be gone. His two-month quest to find Van Blackman would
be over. Riley Martelli took one more long look at the man
in his sights then lowered the weapon.

He could never kill someone in cold blood. Not even
the man who'd murdered his sister and put his six-year-
old nephew, Asher, in the hospital with a bullet lodged
near his spine.

Van knelt, but Riley couldn't see what he was doing.
Soon, small puffs of smoke drifted from the patch of
ground.

Riley settled the gun back on his shoulder and got a
better look with the scope. Van crouched over the small
flame, pushing the contents as though trying to encourage
a larger blaze. Riley lowered the weapon again.

Now, in a very secluded area of Colorado's Rocky
Mountain National Park, Van moved to stand next to a
black SUV just a few yards ahead of him.

It might be July in Colorado, but it was cold at night, dropping into the forties. Van wore a black ski cap pulled low over his ears, but his height and broad shoulders were harder to disguise. Riley's heart pounded. Finally, he was going to bring his sister's killer to justice. He shifted the rifle on his shoulder for one more look through the scope. He scanned his prey's body.

His target turned and Riley now had a full-on view of his face—and his heart stuttered.

It wasn't Van Blackman.

Disappointment shot through him. He had the wrong man. Riley lowered the rifle with a frustrated sigh. Then frowned and lifted it to stare through the scope once again. The man's face was familiar. Where had he seen him before? Television? Yeah, that was it. Could it be— He focused again.

Yep. That was the missing FBI agent who had been all over the news lately. Morrow was his last name. Jake Morrow. And there was a hundred thousand dollars being offered as a reward for his safe return.

Don't miss
BOUNTY HUNTER by Lynette Eason,
available wherever
Love Inspired® Suspense books and ebooks are sold.

www.LoveInspired.com

*Nell Stoltzfus falls for the new local veterinarian in town,
James Pierce. But their love is forbidden since he's
English and she's Amish. If Nell follows her heart,
will love conquer all?*

*Read on for a sneak preview of
A SECRET AMISH LOVE by* **Rebecca Kertz**,
available July 2017 from Love Inspired!

"You said your *bruder* was called out on an emergency,"
Nell said. "What does he do?"

"He's a veterinarian. He's recently opened a clinic here
in Happiness."

The strange sensation settled over Nell. Despite the
difference in their last names, could James be Maggie's
brother? "What's his name?" she asked.

"James Pierce." Maggie smiled. "He owns Pierce
Veterinary Clinic. Have you heard of him?"

"*Ja.* In fact, 'twas your bruder who treated my dog,
Jonas."

"Then you've met him!" Maggie looked delighted. "Is he
a *gut* veterinarian?"

Startled by this new knowledge, Nell could only nod
at first. "He was wonderful with Jonas. He's a kind and
compassionate man." She studied Maggie and recognized
the family resemblance. "How is he a Pierce and you a
Troyer?"

"I am a Pierce." Maggie grinned. "Abigail is, too. But
we don't go by the Pierce name. Adam is our stepfather,

and he is our *dat* now." Maggie's eyes filled with sadness. "I was too young to care, but James had a hard time with it. He loved Dad, and he'd wanted to be a veterinarian like him since he was ten. He became more determined to follow in Dad's footsteps."

Nell felt her heart break for James, who must have suffered after his father's death. "You chose the Amish life, but James chose a different path."

"And he's doing well," Maggie said. "My family is thrilled that he set up his practice in Happiness."

Later that afternoon, James arrived to spend time with his family.

She recognized his car immediately as he drove into the barnyard. James stood a moment, searching for family members. Nell couldn't move as he crossed the yard to where tables and bench seats had been set up. Soon, James headed to the gathering of young people, including his sisters Maggie and Abigail.

Nell found it heartwarming to see that his siblings regarded him with the same depth of love and affection. James spoke briefly to Maggie, clearly delighted that he'd handled his emergency then decided to come. She heard the siblings teasing and the ensuing laughter. Maggie said something to James as she gestured in Nell's direction.

James saw her, and Nell froze. Her heart started to beat hard when he broke away from the group to approach her.

Don't miss
A SECRET AMISH LOVE
by Rebecca Kertz, available July 2017 wherever
Love Inspired® books and ebooks are sold.

www.LoveInspired.com